SHEPHERD'S FIRE

APOCALYPSE CHRONICLES
BOOK 1

DARREL SPARKMAN

ROUGH
EDGES
PRESS

Rough Edges Press
An Imprint of Wolfpack Publishing
9850 S. Maryland Parkway, Suite A-5 #323
Las Vegas, Nevada 89183

roughedgespress.com

Paperback ISBN 978-1-68549-270-0
eBook ISBN 978-1-68549-269-4
LCCN 2023932735

SHEPHERD'S FIRE

PROLOGUE

DIMITRI KUMARIN WAS A KILLER. It didn't matter that no one liked him. What he had was respect. When his bosses had a human resources problem, they called him. Problem gone. He never missed.

But now he was off the books. He hated his cousin for calling in an unsanctioned favor. If the family found out, both their lives might be forfeited. For his part, debts must be paid and his cousin had helped him on occasion. Probably for just this contingency. It was how things were done. Dimitri Kumarin was more at home in St. Louis and Chicago where he could blend into the crowds of people. He needed to be anonymous and invisible in his line of work. And he was not a lover of nature. In his world the trees were concrete and ground carpeted.

But here he was, laying in the weeds and rain waiting for some schmuck to appear so he could put a lead projectile through his head. The visibility was bad and surroundings dismal, but the range was only a hundred yards or so. The weather was just a minor distraction this close to the target. The gun he used was supplied by

Viktor and supposed to be zeroed in at a hundred. He assumed Viktor's supplier was reliable.

And the instructions he'd been given? Have no identification on him. No nothing, so he'd left everything in a motel room in Springfield, MO. He'd chance getting pulled over out in podunkville as he traveled between the town and the hit. If he got caught, nothing should lead back to the family.

He snorted, scanning the back deck of the lake home through the scope. Like he'd ever get caught. He'd been doing this for years and hadn't got popped yet. His rifle was top of the line, a Remington .308 with Leopold scope and suppressor. With the 220-grain subsonic round he was using, it would be relatively quiet. All things considered, he'd like to take it home with him. His instructions were to drop it in the lake after the deed was done. Maybe he would. Maybe he wouldn't. Although, the thought of crossing Viktor sucked his balls up into his belly. That man was cold and crazy.

The family called him Shooter. It was his code name and he liked it better than Dimitri. Only famous in a few circles, his cousin kept him in money and women—and anonymity. It was easy money. Gone were the days that you walked up to someone on a crowded street and shot them in the back of the head, did a home invasion in the middle of the night, or shot up their car. It was much safer all around, except for the victim, to pick an elevated position and do the deed. Collateral damage was not a consideration.

Viktor would leave him the GPS location of a vehicle, usually a top-of-the-line SUV, maybe a Yukon or Suburban. Once he picked up the vehicle, a set of coordinates would lead him to another location to pick up more instructions. Name, location, Google Earth maps, and a picture of the target.

He scanned the back porch as his mind wandered. Only one other member of the family held a better reputation. He'd never met her and didn't want to. Most didn't survive the introduction. Not that he couldn't handle himself. He took his hand off the rifle and checked the pistol positioned for easy access next to the rifle. It was a cheap nine-mil, maybe Chinese or Czech. He didn't care. He took pride in his proficiency with anything that went bang.

So, here he lay among the ticks and chiggers, decked out in the latest ghillie suit of woodland camo and waiting for his target to appear in his fog-shrouded crosshairs. It had better be soon. He had to piss.

ONE

JIM LANE APPROACHED his cabin on the shore of Stockton Lake and paused mid-step at the bottom landing of his back deck. He gazed past the rocky shore toward the water and surrounding forest, a landscape shrouded by mist and fog alternating with each gust of wind. He'd been uneasy all morning—didn't like it, couldn't explain it. Eyes narrowed under a dripping hat brim, he watched a rain shower move through the trees, driven by winds that chilled him and awakened buried memories. A silent dance of ghosts and shadows pushed his mind into places better left alone.

He turned his face to the wind. The water peppering him was an inconvenience along with the feeling of spiders racing up and down his spine. Impatient fingers moved to the butt of his pistol worn in a belly holster. His hand lingered on the rubberized grip with the familiarity of a lover's touch while he sought the unknown catalyst for his uneasiness. But no reassurance appeared in the rain-clouded landscape. A quiet whisper in his mind told him something was out there. The uneasy feeling in his stomach said he couldn't find it.

A deep, cleansing breath offered some calm and he shook his head at his own antsy nerves. This was lake country in southwest Missouri, not a damned jungle in Central America. Get a grip.

He paused a moment to clean mud from his boots before he trudged up the rough planked wooden steps leading to the back deck of his cabin. The front was built on level ground, facing away from the lake. The rear deck stood twenty feet above the dense rocks, scrub brush, and saplings. The ground fell away sharply toward the water making the deck an observation point overlooking a small inlet and the lake beyond.

It was a beautiful view and most days he could see for miles. Today it was wet and cold, and the limited visibility made him claustrophobic.

He and Boney, his fearless black and tan hound, had been tracking wild boar all morning and both were worn out and dragging tail. The panting dog settled on the deck floor, impossibly long tongue hanging to the side while soft brown eyes watched alertly for any sign of a treat being offered.

Jim leaned his shotgun against the rail and hung his floppy bushman's hat over the barrel. Snagging a bottle of water from an outside mini-fridge, he dropped onto one of his deck chairs. His grumbling stomach led him to think about what possibilities there were for lunch as he drained the bottle with a contented sigh.

Boney sidled up to sit beside him and he noticed the dog still wore his cut-vest. The leather contraption helped protect the dog if he tangled with a boar, otherwise their razor-like tusks would rip through his chest like a hot knife through butter. After the mandatory ear scratching and assuring him he was a good dog, he unbuckled the vest and smiled as the dog gratefully bounded away to roll in the wet grass.

With a tired sigh, he watched the wind push rain across the water below, painting lines on a lake surface that was non-reflective and gray as a Navy battleship.

Forty years old—didn't feel a day over sixty. He'd noticed a few gray hairs when he looked in the mirror this morning. Where'd the time go? A short two years ago, he was full of piss and vinegar with his pockets full of cash and ready to take on the world. Today, soaked and tired, a nap was the most exciting thing in his future.

He leaned forward, starting to stand when the top of the porch rail in front of him exploded. It was simple reflex that toppled him backward with a face full of splinters and splattered water. It took him a moment to realize what happened because he didn't hear a shot.

During a stunned few seconds of shocked denial, staring at the ceiling, he watched a dirt dauber wasp investigate a spot for a mud hotel while his mind caught up with what just happened. He'd been shot at before but didn't expect it at his quiet cabin on the lake. A quick look revealed Boney watching him with interest but no more than any dog looking at a crazy acting human. Jim came out of his momentary shock feeling a sting where the bullet grazed his shoulder. What the hell?

Another bullet ripped any thought of an accidental or errant round from a hunter as it slammed through his hat. The shotgun clattered to the floor and the hat left a wet mark on the wall behind him—right next to a bullet hole. His Boonie hat lay on the deck with a hole in it and held the condom that had covered the end of the shotgun barrel.

He didn't hear that shot either, just felt the jarring slap of the bullet punching through the siding on his cabin. When he realized someone was shooting at him personally with a suppressed rifle, that pissed him off. A suppressed rifle isn't silent, but with distance it may as well be.

Trying to calm his nerves, he stayed immobile. The shooter couldn't see him, or that second shot would have been in him, not his hat. Someone searching the deck of his house through a scope would pick up movement quickly, but would have tunnel vision. The high magnification of the scope limits field of view, which was why most snipers used someone to help, a spotter. Without a spotter, the shooter is reduced to a one or two-shot wonder.

The shooter had to be directly across the water, which would put them only a couple hundred yards away. The splintered rail was almost level with the hole in his wall so the shooter was straight across. With the rain and fog, there was no hope of finding the location by any smoke from the rifle. There wouldn't be much anyway.

Looking up at the gouge in the banister and then at the hole behind him, he knew he was lucky to be alive. He also felt the shooter was good, but not great. Any of the local hunters would have spit a stream of their favorite smokeless tobacco to the side, and then left his carcass sliding down the wall along with his hat, although a hundred-yard shot on a rainy and windy day wasn't easy.

Anger clouded any thoughts of why someone shot at him, and he tried to push it down. He knew the best way to defeat any opponent was to first make them mad, and lately, he'd had some anger management issues. After a couple of deep breaths, his mind cleared.

The problem was easy when reduced to a simple equation. Someone shot at him. That had to stop. He would find out why later.

When no more rounds came his way and using the overturned chair for added cover, he crawled along the wall and around the corner of the wrap-around deck of his cabin.

Checking the Glock .40 caliber pistol in his belt holster, something he carried all the time thanks to Missouri's open carry law, he eased into the house and avoided the windows. He thought of calling 911, but the shooter would likely be gone by the time the cavalry arrived. If not, it could put some overzealous and under trained deputy in harm's way. None would be trained to go against an active shooter in the woods. Problem was... they would think they were, and that would get them dead.

Jim sighed. This problem was his and his alone. It had been a few years, but the skills weren't gone. A little rusty...well, maybe a lot rusty.

As he went out the front door, he grabbed a couple of loaded fifteen-round magazines for his pistol and then faded into the forest. The shotgun would have been handy, but it was in plain sight on the back deck, and he was afraid the shooter would notice it missing. He had some long guns in a wall safe, along with a decked-out M-4, but quickly dismissed that idea. They weren't worth much in the close confines of woods and scrub brush. And he was used to his pistol.

A flicker of movement to his right let him know

Boney was shadowing him. There was no time to tie him up, and the dog had never responded to hand signals anyway, other than grin at him with his tongue hanging out.

The cabin was between him and the shooter, at least if the shooter didn't move. Knowing the terrain across from his cabin, there was only one good spot for a shooter to be. He ran hard about fifty yards into the forest and away from the lake before he turned left. A half mile of walking would get him to a place he could come up behind the shooter's location.

The inlet separating him and the shooter ended a short distance from his house so he could cross the shallow end of the gorge and start his approach. The low visibility would give them both cover, no advantage either way. Given that they'd missed twice made him think the assailant might make another mistake and stay in one spot.

A game trail offered a quick approach to the other side of the gorge. He avoided a footbridge as being too noisy and exposed. Once across and into the trees, he moved slowly, allowing his breathing to slow down. Without the rain poncho, his mottled and faded green cotton shirt left him shivering in the cold drizzle but allowed him to blend in with the forest around him.

Boney trotted up to him, nudged against his leg a moment and then moved away on silent feet. He watched curiously until the dog faded from view. Guess he was saying howdy.

About fifty yards from the area he thought the shooter would place himself, he stopped behind a tree, pulling his pistol from its holster. The rubberized and checkered grip repelled moisture and felt solid in his hand like the well-worn tool it was. The Glock .40 cal wasn't pretty but would always shoot whether it was dirty or clean. He wished he'd grabbed a cap to keep the rain out of his eyes, but there was no use worrying about that now.

He wove a quiet path through the fern, patches of sumac, and waist-high weeds, drifting through fog that shrouded the landscape like some B-rated horror flick. Thunder grumbled in the distance and the rain increased, falling straight down like a tropical shower, hissing through the overhead leaves. For the moment, the wind had stopped.

Stepping carefully on rain-soaked leaves, avoiding any loose rocks or limbs that would make noise, it took him a few moments to be directly across from his cabin and at a slightly higher level. This was a spot he would choose if circumstances were reversed. He stood relaxed and silent next to an old oak that was at least three feet wide.

He spared a glance at the tree next to him, making sure a copperhead wasn't nestled in the bark. They dearly loved tree frogs and the rough, deep-grooved bark made easy climbing for them—or slithering. With that thought, he took a careful, slow step away from the tree.

The quick shower moved on and the rain became a mist. A strong breeze started at treetop level, and then he felt it against his cheeks. The fog was dissipating, dropping water from the leaves like tiny, guided missiles aimed for the collar of his shirt, coursing cold water down his spine.

Every instinct and sense told him someone was on the slope below. Methodically, starting close and then expanding the area, he began to search for the shooter. He'd learned long ago to look at things specifically when searching—the shadow beside a moss-covered boulder, the way a bush moved in the breeze, or scuff marks in the leaves.

Water dripped from the trees with another wind gust, peppering the floor of the forest with the pitter-patter of liquid feet. His pulse thrummed loudly in his ears. It took all his willpower not to take a deep breath to relieve the tension—to not move. A crow called in the distance, and he heard a wren fussing in the bushes behind him. Another gust of wind moved through the trees as he waited, thunder grumbled in the distance. The ghosts and shadows were back and assailed his senses with memories of other days...other forests—jungles. It was a distraction he didn't need, but hard to push away.

TWO

HE FINALLY SAW the shooter about twenty feet in front of him, slightly downhill and lying on a piece of level ground next to a clump of sumac and poke berry. He wore a green camouflage ghillie suit and if the shooter hadn't moved his foot, he'd have remained hidden. It was like one of those puzzles where something is in plain sight but you can't see it. Once Jim saw movement, the shooter materialized in stark relief. And he appeared to be alone.

A rifle, with the barrel wrapped in camouflage tape, rested on a bipod and pointed toward the cabin. He could see the shooter move the barrel left and right, using the scope to scan the area and try to acquire a target. The shooter must have been frustrated, or the nervous foot wouldn't have happened.

The man was too locked in on his sight picture, with no situational awareness, because Boney was sitting about twenty feet to his side trying to imitate a pointer—couldn't fault him for trying. He was pretty sure a bird dog wouldn't have his tongue hanging out laughing.

All doubts about the situation fell away. He'd seen enough. Someone wanted him dead. Whether the shooter was male or female, young or old just didn't matter anymore. It was time for some answers. In the movies the good guy would disarm the shooter by sneaking up behind them and putting a pistol behind their ear—that would get you killed.

The silence was so peaceful Jim hated to break it— steeled himself against the coming noise. Although he felt it wouldn't work, he spoke from cover. "Don't move."

The man in front of him flinched, hands gripping tightly on the rifle.

Well, maybe it would work. "I want you to shove the rifle away from you, and then stand up real slow. I'm sure you know the drill."

Pushing the rifle forward against the bipod mount proved fruitless, so the shooter just shoved the butt of the rifle away. He came to his knees and then stood facing away from Jim.

"Alright. Turn around and show me your hands."

When the man turned, he held a pistol in his hand, not quite bringing it level before he stopped, gaze held tightly on Jim's gun.

"Unless you're in a hurry to die, we need to talk." Jim moved a step to his right, giving him a better angle and increasing the distance the shooter would have to swing his pistol to bring it on target. Inches count.

"Don't think so." The man spoke finally. "You holding that gun one-handed means we have about even odds. I don't think you can hit shit at this distance."

"I wouldn't bet your life on that." Jim shrugged. "Why did you shoot at me?"

The man smirked. "That's a stupid question. Somebody wants you dead."

"It's always that simple, isn't it?" Jim nodded and gave a resigned sigh. "Okay, so we're down to it. I could do something dramatic like telling you the next sound you hear is the click of my safety being disengaged, or give you some other warning. Like in the movies. But I'm holding a Glock, so that's out the window. It's always packed and racked. Last chance to talk this out."

The shooter grinned before speaking, giving Jim a calculating glance. "Not a chance. I can beat you, old man. This ain't going to be much of a gunfight."

Jim's gaze never wavered from the shooter's eyes. "Well, that was just plain hurtful. For your information, us old people were taught a different way. You don't get old by being slow."

Every new generation is prideful...better than the one they're replacing, or so they think. Jim felt it was going the other way. Humankind was losing a little every day, bit by bit failing to see what they'd never recover.

The shooter was mocking, confident. "So we do it like the cowboys in the Old West?"

"I don't think they liked being called cowboy, but yeah, something like that."

The silence stretched out. He saw the shooter's expression change and knew it was coming—tried to derail it. Knew it was fruitless.

"It's your choice. You don't have to die."

The shooter's stare turned hot and feverish, weighing his chances—his earlier confident smile dropped to a grimace.

Jim sighed, making his mind and body quiet, waiting for the inevitable, finally nodding to the man. "I'm taking up slack."

The shooter was good. Jim hadn't finished the words before two shots rocketed at him from the shooter's handgun. Both bullets thudded into the tree beside him, throwing splinters into his side. His answering shot was center mass and backed the shooter up. The man tripped over his rifle to land awkwardly on his back. The man convulsed, coughed, and then tried to raise his pistol for another shot. One more round found its mark above the shooter's left eyebrow.

Moving to the other side of the huge tree, Jim waited several moments. The man was right. He'd been faster. He glanced at the tree. Every inch counts. As he looked around, he noticed Boney had disappeared.

Finally, he walked to the man and nudged him with his foot. It was a mindless gesture. The man was dead. Kneeling, he lifted the edge of the ghillie suit and saw a ballistic vest. This little bit of insurance must have been why the man was so cocky. It had to be a level IIA or level III to stop his forty cal, but the shooter probably had never been shot and wasn't ready for the physical punch. You don't get to practice getting shot. Though there was little penetration, it still knocked him down, probably cracked some ribs—not that he'd lived to worry about it.

Looking around for any sign of a partner or spotter and seeing none, he holstered his gun. They'd have been next to each other if he had a partner. Usually it irritated him that he'd not thought of that before he engaged the shooter. Still rusty.

Who the hell was this? Looking at the forest around him, his hearing deafened by the two shots from the shooter and the deeper cough of his own gun, the bigger question came back to nag him.

Why? What had the shooter said? Someone wanted

him dead. The rifle and ghillie suit spoke of money. And all things can be had for money.

He looked at the man lying in the weeds with little passion or remorse. All things considered, he'd rather have had a better discussion about who he was and why he was here, but his eventual demise was predestined. Nobody gets to try and kill you and then walks away. And shooting to wound? Not when your adversary is shooting at you. There was only one outcome. One of you dies.

And the why was obvious. Like the man said, somebody wanted him dead. This was just a soldier, sent to do a job. Now the opportunity to question the man was gone, unless there was something on his body to give a clue.

The rifle looked new and was a popular Remington .308. There would be a hundred just like it in local gun cabinets. However, that was the only thing about the rifle that was normal.

The bipod was a standard, but rarely seen option. The suppressor screwed on the front of the barrel was not normal. It wasn't illegal in Missouri, but highly restricted. Deer hunters don't need suppressed rifles, although he'd thought of it when hunting Big Red. The scope was a Leopold and that meant big bucks—bucks as in money, not deer. The adjustable stock had an ammo sleeve that originally held five cartridges. There were three missing and he assumed the single shot rifle held a round. Looking at them, he surmised they were the subsonic 220 grain and the reason he didn't hear the rounds fired at him. He cleared the rifle and placed the round with the others.

Jim looked next to the body and found the two expended casings. After pocketing them, he returned to the tree he'd stood by, searched a moment through the wet grass and then retrieved his own brass. There was no telling what would come of this. He might as well be careful. The two bullet holes in the tree stayed. He used his knife to make the holes look more like trail markings or cuts to the bark, found an old piece of wood and rubbed it on the fresh cuts, staining the fresh-cut wood to look old.

Returning to the body, he found a new holster for the nine-millimeter pistol clipped to the shooter's belt, and the nine-mil screamed city boy. Some of the locals would consider that a girl's gun or something a gangbanger from the inner city would carry. On the other hand, it was the most popular handgun caliber in the US and there were a lot out there.

He couldn't find any kind of knife, not even a folding pocketknife. Who goes out into the woods without a knife? Jim had two on him now; a folding knife with a serrated blade and a boot knife with a bone handle and stainless-steel blade. A knife was a tool and not for show. Locally, no one over nine years old would make that mistake.

This man was good at what he did, but not country good. He was out of his element. It was an assumption but he felt it was accurate. Now, why would an amateur city boy be shooting at him?

Turning his attention to the body, he noted all the clothes looked new. The pockets were empty and the shirt was a brand he'd seen at Walmart. He could buy the ghillie suit and tactical vest online, or in any outdoor store like Bass Pro or Cabela's.

What bothered him—well, one of many things—was the obvious attempt to be anonymous. He'd bet the man memorized the phone number of his lawyer. The tactic was simple. Say nothing. Call a lawyer to get out of jail if caught. Make bail. Disappear.

Why try to fight when caught? That made no sense, along with the rest of the situation. Even so, the man had come damned close to putting holes in him. It was another question with no answers. He needed to go play lotto. A man obviously intent on killing him had shot four times and missed. It doesn't get any luckier than that.

He didn't recognize the man but doubted he'd recognize anyone after a head shot with a .40 caliber hollow point.

None of this made sense. He didn't have the kind of money that was worth killing for, nor did he hold title to any land that would need a quit-claim deed bought with a bullet. He shook his head.

What the hell?

———

SQUATTING NEXT TO THE BODY, he tried to reason it out. There might be enemies in his past, and some might have a far enough reach to cause trouble. The Shepherds, his most recent employer, could help weed them out, but he'd walked away from them and was off their radar—wasn't sure he wanted to make contact.

Mostly, people in his past wouldn't think he was worth the hassle. None would know his identity, although he supposed it was possible. With enough money, no information is safe. Up to a few weeks ago, he'd had a good couple of years. With the money saved from his contract work, he was enjoying life. It was slow and boring until now, just like he wanted it. What was the old saying? A mystery wrapped in an enigma wrapped in a mystery.

Looking around to make sure the shooting hadn't attracted any attention, he felt relieved to find the forest deserted. At least, what he could see of it. The rain would muffle the sound of most gunshots to a half mile or less. Finding nothing that would help him identify the man, he rolled him in his suit and slung him over his shoulder. Thankful the shooter was a small man, he picked up the rifle and walked off through the forest. He'd take him to the hole.

As he walked across the forest floor, pausing often to rest and figure out the easiest way, he again considered calling 911. It was a fleeting thought, because this man had put an effort into being invisible. There was a small chance his fingerprints would be on file, but he found that unlikely unless the man was military or had been a guest of the penal system.

Regardless, the man wasn't wearing gloves, so prints would be on the rifle. Jim's reluctance to involve law enforcement stemmed from the certainty that when he found out who sent the shooter, and he would find out, the law wouldn't condone his response and be a definite hindrance. Besides, the adage was true. When seconds count, local law enforcement is minutes away. It wasn't their fault. They couldn't be everywhere at once. But the statistic was true just the same. So, most country folk had the philosophy of the Castle Doctrine. Only, each person is a castle, most were armed and would rather be judged by twelve than carried by six.

He repositioned the dead weight on his shoulders, wishing he'd gone to get his four-wheeler and a rope. But, as soon as he thought of it he discounted the idea. Dragging a corpse would leave a trail, a whole lot of trail. Not to mention the engine noise attracting the attention of anyone in the area.

Twenty minutes later the midday sun tried to peek through the clouds and the temperature rose, pushing the humidity toward levels that were more in the boiling sauna range. Winded, he finally kneeled on legs turning to jelly and dropped the body next to a thin, limestone slab about the size of a car door. He moved the leaves and sticks that covered the rock.

Resting a moment, trying to catch his breath, he vowed to start working out. Sweat and the shooter's blood soaked his clothes. He listened and scanned his surroundings. Only natural sounds came from the forest. Other than the barking squirrels and an occasional sharp cry from a blue jay, he was alone.

Hell, no one was stupid enough to be out on a day like this. That is, except for him and the shooter. He stood and grasped the slab, dragging it sideways to reveal a hole under the limestone about three feet across. Cool, stagnant air wafted out of the opening. The hole wasn't round, more of a jagged rectangle, so he had to be careful with the covering—and himself. The sides were rounded and worn smooth from...well, a lot of things falling through over the years.

When he first moved to the area, he'd been following a deer. It had been a good shot, but deer with punctured lungs or heart will still run a good distance. The bleeding animal left an easy trail. Staggering away about fifty yards ahead of him, it disappeared. He'd carefully approached the last spot he saw the deer. Careful because no one wants to step on a wounded deer thrashing around. It was a good way to get hurt. What he discovered was the hole, almost stepping into it himself.

Curious, he dropped rocks down into the darkness and never heard them hit bottom. On one occasion, he brought three hundred feet of nylon rope, tied a rock to the end of it and lowered it into the hole. It never touched bottom and the rock came back dry. As a safety measure, he dragged in a flat, thin rock to cover the opening.

He dumped the body into the cavernous grave, shucked out of his shirt and pants, and tossed them into the hole. It was lucky blood hadn't dripped on his boots. He liked his boots. Looking at the shooter's pistol for a moment, he disassembled it and tossed the pieces after the body. It was a cheap gun and a throwaway. The pistol wasn't worth saving, but he kept the rifle. He had plans for that. Now there was nothing to tie him to the death of this man except for a rifle he'd bet wasn't registered anywhere.

Finished, he slid and pushed the flat rock cover back into place. After kicking leaves and sticks on the rock and around it, he strode toward his cabin praying that no one would see him because the whole world was equipped with cell phone cameras now. Parents even gave toddlers toy phones just to get them ready for the real thing.

So, here he was. Just a new fashion statement of a near-naked man in boxer shorts and knee-high boots strolling through the forest, carrying his belt and pistol, along with a new sniper rifle. Nothing to see here. Nope. Move along, folks.

Shit, what a mess.

THREE

LIMESTONE COUNTY SHERIFF Rita Morris sat in her faded silver Jeep Cherokee, drumming the fingers of her left hand on the steering wheel while the other gripped her pistol. She contemplated the vehicle parked in front of her. The situation brought back too many nightmares. Telling herself there was nothing to worry about didn't work. When you can't believe your own thoughts, who can you trust? A couple of practiced, measured breaths brought her heart rate close to normal. Sort of.

About to turn on an access lane that led down to the lake for a little fishing and relaxation, she'd spied a vehicle pulled off the road into the high grass that bordered the forest.

Cursing her luck for a moment, thinking about the comfort of the covered pier she used on occasion, she pulled in behind the vehicle. It sat next to a one-lane country road that skirted a ridge overlooking a southern fork of Lake Stockton. She cycled her windshield wipers for a better view.

The black Suburban SUV with dark tinted windows didn't fit. It looked like one of the President's protection detail had lost a car—it shouldn't be here. Plus, no license plate on the back. Not unheard of or illegal, but still odd. Coupled with the kind of vehicle it was, very odd.

This was not a hunter's vehicle. Hunters used pickups or older vehicles they didn't mind having blood and mud in, not a brand new slicked-up Suburban.

She couldn't see any movement within the vehicle. No one came from the surrounding woods even after she beeped the horn a couple of times.

A nauseating knot of fear grew in her belly, expanding into her chest. Her breath became shallow and she focused on her breathing to prevent hyperventilation. In the span of a few moments, she'd gone from deep breathing to a shallow breaths that wouldn't disturb a dust particle. Dammit, why couldn't she control her thoughts? She didn't need this. Not now. Not ever.

It was hot and rainy, a prelude to a typical muggy Missouri day. People complaining they could cut the humidity with a knife weren't necessarily wrong. Fog shrouded the area and memories clouded her mind. *The* memory. The memory of her husband being killed in the line of duty. Like thousands of policemen do every day, he'd walked up to a pickup truck during a routine traffic stop on a day like this. Knowing him, she was sure he'd been in a good mood, ready to joke with the speeder and let them go with a warning to be careful. He wrote very few tickets. Instead, the occupant fired several rounds through the vehicle's door.

Sheriff Johnny Morris died that day, living long

enough to radio that he was down and give a description of the truck. A day just like today. Rainy. Gloomy. A good day for being inside.

The shooter was caught soon after and didn't survive the take-down. He'd been wounded by his own ricochet —slugs go through the thin walls of vehicles like a hot knife through butter. Except for the parts that aren't thin.

The apprehension followed an unwritten law with country folk—the hand of justice strikes swiftly and without the need for a lot of legal intervention when it's one of their own. Johnny was respected. No one was saying whether it was a law enforcement officer or private citizen with a police-band radio who dropped the man. It wasn't important. The shooter needed to be dead. He was dead.

Drugs were found in the truck after a search and they figured the driver panicked when he got stopped. Most said he went for a weapon, even the ones that weren't there. Still, she'd liked to have had a few minutes with him. Alone. Call it closure.

Rita sighed, once again trying to get her breathing under control. God, she missed him—missed the soft touches, his hands on her skin...he could always calm her with a look or smile. She could still smell him when he hugged her. Some memories just don't go away. Emotional loss has PTSD too.

She glanced at the car again. Pull up your big girl panties and get it done! She blinked back tears as she reached for the door handle with shaky fingers.

The low crackling of the radio startled her. Dammit. What now? Her vacation started today.

"Three twenty-five, Limestone."

She thought about ignoring it, but the 325-call indicated her specifically. Even on vacation she was still the sheriff. Keeping her attention on the vehicle in front of her, she picked up and keyed the handset.

"Go, Limestone."

The dispatcher was an older woman in her sixties with a voice that would do well on a phone sex line. She knew Agnes was a grandmother ten times over and about as unflappable as anyone she'd ever seen. She was also Rita's mother confessor and friend.

"*Ten twenty-one.*"

Hmmm. Curious. Now what? The ten code that law enforcement departments sometimes used was asking her for a call back. None were universal and often were modified as more military people were hired. Since everyone and their uncle had a monitor with EMS bands, she kept it short. Her response was immediate, if incorrect, acknowledging the call.

"K."

"*Limestone clear. Fourteen twenty-two.*"

Her attention divided between the SUV and surrounding area, she pulled her cell phone from her shirt pocket and speed dialed Agnes.

"What's up? Why the hell didn't you just call my cell?"

The sound of a yawn came through the phone. "Just going by the book. You never know when some overzealous prosecutor will review the tapes. Besides, I didn't want to disturb you. You know, like if you were out of the vehicle chasing Mr. Right with your fishing pole. Those are the rules, girlie. You call me on your personal phone, I don't call you."

"Oh, all right. I give up. Always hitting me with rules and crap. So, what's so important you'd interrupt the first day of my vacation?"

Rita was looking at the forest around her, not wanting any surprises popping out of the bushes. Given the choice, she didn't want surprises anywhere. Anytime. Well, maybe...flowers on occasion...

The honey-dripping voice ignored her interruption. "I just got a piece of news to pass on to you and then I'll let you go. A certain hunky individual is sitting at his lake house on this fabulous, beautiful day in Limestone County and wishing you'd give him a call. When he called and asked for you specifically, he made it low key, but it sounded semi-important. A free bit of advice? I've heard he got rid of that Ruskie woman, so you need to see about taking that boy off the market, sweetie. ASAP. There's no point in you shriveling on the vine...so to speak."

She got another knot in her stomach that had nothing to do with fear and pushed down the almost smile trying to take over her face. Shriveling indeed.

"C'mon, Agnes. How do you know about his girl-friend? You must have spies behind every tree in the four-state area—"

She flinched and then focused on movement to her left. An armadillo, locally known as an opossum-on-a-half-shell, waddled out from under a pile of brush, paused a moment wiggling its ears and then went back the way it came.

"—but thanks for the heads-up. For your information, I knew this a couple of weeks ago. One of the girls at the Lakehouse Café said he canceled a reservation. Of course, the nosy-nellie had to ask him why." She paused a moment. "Did he say what he wanted?"

Agnes laughed outright. "Nope, very mysterious. He just said to please call."

"Look." Rita tried to make her voice stern, but it was hard to do with Agnes. "Since I'm on *vacation...*" She stressed the last word. "Have a couple of the guys come and check out this SUV I'm parked behind." She gave directions to the area. "Something isn't right out here, so have them use caution. I don't see plates, so they'll have to get the VIN. If it's Barney, make sure he brings a magnifying glass. He can't see the end of his own nose."

She could hear Agnes responding to another call on her radio, and then she was back, sighing into her ear.

"You're behind an SUV that's pulled over? Now, I get it. Honey, you know that was a fluke that happened to Johnny. A one in a million chance. You need to find a way to let that go. It's been a year. Girl, you need to get out and find a life for yourself."

"I know you think that, Agnes. Hell, that's all I ever hear. 'It was nobody's fault. Just one of those things. Move on.' Live your life. But you know what? He played the lotto for years and never won. And now? You're saying he hit a million to one long shot? Luck like that I don't need and neither does anyone else. It never hurts to be careful. That's what I aim to be. Careful."

Memories of that day bubbled up to the surface of her mind, but she pushed them down. She started the engine on her Cherokee. "I'm pretty close to the lake house. I'll just wander on by. Who knows? I might get invited to a fish fry, or something."

Agnes chuckled. "Right. Just don't wander too much. And if you do, me and the girls will want a full report tomorrow." There was silence on the phone—neither had hung up. "So, have you decided yet?"

Her mother confessor never missed a trick. She'd often wondered if she should use Agnes while interrogating low-level offenders. Some teenager trying to hide that he'd boosted a car? Not possible. No one could resist her.

"Yeah, I've decided. I'm not going to run for office. My heart's just not in it anymore. You must be psychic. It was only a few minutes ago that I figured out that I don't like this job."

The soft voice was sympathetic. "And cars parked by the roadside?"

"Yeah. I've found that I really don't care much for cars parked by the roadside, or traffic stops in general. I suppose it's a coward's way out, but that's the way I feel about it—and that's how I'm going to play it. When I pull in behind a car, I have a pucker factor you couldn't drive a pencil through with a hammer. I can't feel that way and do my job." She ran her fingers through her hair and sighed. "Look, thanks for the heads up. I'd better go."

"Hey, sis." Agnes's voice turned into full mother mode. "You got no one to please but yourself. And, for what it's worth? I think you've made the right decision. You're still young enough to start a family and do girlie stuff. You don't need to be cowboy tough just because your husband was."

The call ended but the "what-ifs" bouncing around in her mind did not. What would the future bring for an unemployed widow of a county sheriff, an appointed acting sheriff, and ex-deputy? What does that description get you on the job market? Walking security somewhere? Driving an armored car?

And she'd have to read up on girlie stuff. She hadn't felt girlie in a long time—couldn't imagine waking up next to someone in the morning. The last time she looked at her wild-haired image in a mirror, she nearly shot her reflection.

FOUR

RITA DROVE through a tree-canopied lane of hardwood oak and maple. She pulled into a clearing and parked next to a beat-up old Dodge short-bed pickup with a lid on the back. The pickup didn't look like much and had a lot of wear on it, but she knew for a fact it ran like a top. The big Turbo V-8 engine wouldn't be much on gas mileage, but when she heard it go by on the road, it always purred like a kitten.

Much like the effect the man she was about to meet had on women. Even married women get a buzz looking at eye candy occasionally. She chided herself for thinking like that. Though she'd known Jim Lane as an acquaintance through her late husband and liked him, this was strictly business.

She took a moment to re-wrap her long, black hair into a tighter ponytail while she critically studied her face in the rearview mirror. Too many wrinkles. Laugh lines? Too serious an expression. Smiles just make more wrinkles, right? Her sigh was long drawn out. What the hell was she doing?

Looking around, she'd always envied this location. The cabin was a modified A-frame with a perpendicular side addition. Nestled into the surrounding woods, the forest floor was cushioned with pine needles and old oak leaves. The home was hidden enough from the highway to be missed if you weren't looking for it. Even the road to the cabin looked like a fire trail, at least for the part visible from the highway, and she knew that was by design.

Her late husband helped haul in creek gravel for the drive, because it was brown and not likely to be noticed. She'd then watched as Jim meticulously covered the whole driveway in pine needles and old leaves for cover. She wondered about that and asked her husband if Lane was hiding out. The answer was maybe just from himself. As she walked up the front step onto the porch, she heard him yell.

"I'm around back, Rita."

How'd he do that? The man seemed to know every thought of anyone brave enough to step on his property. She navigated the porch that wrapped around the entire house. Jim sat in a chair on the back deck, feet up on the rail and long-necked Bud Light in his hand. There was clearly something on his mind. She'd seen him often enough to know that on a normal day his dark-blue eyes were mocking and humorous, but today his weathered face and expression looked serious.

She reviewed what she knew of him, little that it was —and mentally kicked herself for not checking deeper. That could be remedied with a phone call. She knew he was around forty years old, and she could see a little gray at the temples of the unruly mop of dirty-blond hair. Per local intelligence, he was romantically unattached for the moment. She remembered from brief conversations with her husband that Jim had been military for a while and then worked for a private security company. Neither she nor her husband could find out which one, only that it was highly specialized and not one of the heavy hitters that hired mercenaries. That pretty much left high-level government or private security that did the dirty work the government didn't want to do. Dangerous work.

Past that, her information came to a screeching halt, except for the most important fact. Her husband had liked and respected him. That kind of praise didn't come easy and it told her Jim was a good person and trustworthy. Her husband trusted him, so she would too.

An old and dirty St. Louis Cardinals ball cap perched on the back of his head, worn only the way a country boy could do it. He stood to shake her hand and she took in his lean body clothed in simple jeans and a tee shirt as she held his grip for a long moment. He surprised her by pulling her close and kissing her on the cheek. Unexpected...but not entirely unwelcome.

His ugly dog bounded up and sniffed her legs. She laughed as the odd-looking canine turned and strolled down the steps and disappeared into the brush. "That's some guard dog you have there."

They stood facing one another for a moment past normal before they parted and she wondered what was going on with him. He seemed mad and troubled at the same time. She'd never seen him this edgy. "Are you all right, Jim?"

He released her hand with a lingering touch and returned to his chair. "Not bad. Been better, been worse. If this rain doesn't let up, the lake will be up to my back porch and I'll lose all my koi."

When she leaned over to look at the bright-colored fish in the pool below, she noticed his shotgun leaning against the rail. "Did you try for that big boar again this morning? The red one?"

She knew he'd been trying to thin the feral hogs in the area, a job she approved of since the hogs caused all kinds of grief to the local landowners, and the sheriff's office just didn't have the manpower to deal with them. The Conservation Department had given up a long time ago.

"God, I'd love to get a shot at him," she commented, still trying to draw him out.

Rita watched his reactions closely, but he didn't flinch at the question. Might be the truth, might not be. He was hard to read even for someone like her whose life depended on reading people. Her gaze dropped to the deck floor and his followed as she stared at a condom next to the chair leg.

"Whoops! Sorry. That one got away." He leaned down to grab the errant prophylactic and put it over the barrel of the gun.

She gazed at him a moment. "Right." She couldn't help but arch a brow as she looked closer. "If you'd used large or medium, it wouldn't be loose and come off the barrel."

He smiled at her. "Yeah, but then it'd be hard to get off and I'd have to shoot through it. It's all I had."

She could feel a slow flush creeping up her neck. Why be embarrassed about a condom just because it was his? And Agnes be damned, she was not ready for this.

He continued the conversation like there'd been no interruptions or innuendos. "Saw him. But I couldn't get a clean shot. Wish I had. That big boy has to top out over seven hundred pounds."

She leaned against the rail with arms folded, waiting him out. He clearly wanted to talk about something. She glanced at his ever-present Glock 22 on the table before him next to a loaded magazine and an oiled rag along with a cleaning kit.

One of the things she remembered was that he always carried. Always. Along with the shotgun leaning on the rail, there was a rifle propped up against the house. It was equipped with a scope, bipod attachment, and suppressor. That piqued her interest. Why the hell did he need a suppressor? She hadn't seen any paperwork on that, and it should be filed. All in all, he seemed extremely well-armed for a rainy day conversation.

"Speaking of hunting," he continued, staring out across the lake—anywhere except her eyes. "I found this rifle in the woods this morning."

A cold chill washed over her, sending a shiver across her skin. She really didn't like surprises. And nobody leaves a rifle like that lying around. Nobody. Her first, second, and third thoughts went back to the abandoned SUV.

She couldn't keep the skepticism out of her voice. "Where exactly did this unlikely occurrence take place?"

"Over there." He waved at the woods across the water from them. "It's all decked out like a SWAT rifle. I remembered once someone mentioned your department needed more firepower, but couldn't afford it." He motioned to the Remington leaning against the house. "Besides, I wouldn't want a kid to find it and play with it. I unloaded it."

She pinned him with an intense gaze. Sheriff or not,

her Spidey sense was tripping alarm bells and dancing on the web. Her gaze took in every detail around her as she thought about the SUV being in easy walking distance to the ridge across the water.

The fight or flight instinct is a part of the human condition. For law enforcement it's a feeling that starts as a low buzz in the pit of the stomach and puts every sense on hyper-alert. Her voice was hoarse.

"You found it...like...all by itself?"

FIVE

JIM WATCHED Rita as she leaned against the rail. She carried her six-foot frame with a feline grace that grabbed any male's attention within sight. She'd tied her long black hair up in a ponytail—hair that had a deep luster even in the shade. With her deep-blue eyes, freckles on her cheeks and a spring in her step that showed her athletic history, she about took his breath away.

From her expression, he knew he'd made a mistake. She was looking at him like a mother looks at a four-year-old caught in a lie.

Her voice was hoarse. "You have no idea who owns this rifle?"

"Who owns it? Not a clue." Now he was double-sure trying to fool her was a bad idea. Aside from the guilt from lying to her, which he was sure she could see, she was too damned smart. From the look in her eyes, he was afraid of losing her respect with each word of his misbegotten story. But still, it was the only story he had.

"I thought you might find the owner by dusting it for

prints," he continued. "If the prints aren't on file, and no one comes into your office to claim the gun, I guess it would be yours. I sure don't need it."

The explanation sounded feeble, even to his own ears. Deciding to play it this way was one of those decisions that sound good in the dark, but the light of day destroys the logic.

He watched as she rubbed the gouge in the wood on the railing, seeming to be deep in thought, peeling up a couple of splinters in the process, examining them a moment and then tossing them over the side. She gazed across the water at the woods beyond and then glanced back at him.

From where she stood, the two bullet holes had to be obvious in the log wall behind his chair. Her gaze narrowed as she looked at them. Again, her fingers traced the outline of the gouged rail and then returned to settle on his eyes.

She seemed to have come to a decision. He couldn't tell from her expression if he was going to like it.

"My husband thought of you as a friend. He trusted you." She locked her gaze on his eyes and didn't waver. Her voice was soft. The clouds above the cabin still misted a little. The wind blew just enough to coat her hair with a sheen of moisture. She leaned against the railing, one shoulder on a post, and glanced at the woods across the lake again. She knew he was lying, and she knew the shooter had been in that general direction. Still, she hadn't called him on it.

He nodded. He'd lost friends in combat, and other situations, but what happened with her husband seemed such a damned waste. "I appreciate that. We were friends and what happened to him was just bad luck. He was a damned good man."

"You and everyone else keep telling me that. Just bad luck. Agnes called it one in a million." She gave him a direct stare. "You do realize I'm the sheriff of this county and it's my duty to investigate any crime." Her gaze never wavered. "My duty, Jim. You understand duty?"

He squirmed in his chair, hoping he didn't sound defensive—knowing he did. "What crime would that be? It's no crime to forget and leave your gun in the woods. Stupid? Yes. Maybe the owner saw a snake, or maybe a bear, dropped the gun and ran away." He almost laughed at himself. Now, that really sounded stupid. "I haven't seen it yet, but at night I can hear a cougar. It actually does sound like a woman screaming. I'd heard that but never believed it. Spooky as hell."

She gestured at him to stop, shaking her head. Maybe she didn't like the lies on top of lies. "On the other hand, Johnny always told me to trust you and to let you know if I needed help with anything, especially if I was in danger. He dropped that little nugget of wisdom on me just a few days before he died."

Her voice was low, and she gazed out at the lake again. "I know you've had some military experience, but don't know much else about you. At the time, I wondered why he would imply you are dangerous but could also help me out of any bad situation. Maybe he had a premonition?"

He almost flinched when she looked at him again. Those eyes had sparks in them he'd never seen. And she'd used the word *trust* twice. "What happened out here, Jim? Who took a shot at you?" She looked at the wall behind him and one of her eyebrows rose. "Let's say two shots, to be precise?"

When he didn't answer, her voice turned soft.

"Damn it, Jim. Talk to me."

When he still didn't answer, he watched her turn back toward the lake. She stood ramrod straight and continued looking across the water at the forest beyond and then glanced at him over her shoulder. Her face held a small smile and he still felt like a recalcitrant four-year-old.

"If you're not going to tell me what is going on, then I have to make some wild assumptions here." She waved her hand in a small circle. "Feel free to jump in and interrupt me at any point."

He sighed, wishing he hadn't started this. What the hell was he thinking? He wondered if he could be like Old Red and bust through this trap—a trap of his own making.

"All right, speculate away."

She breathed deep and then turned around to face him. "You wouldn't be sitting here if there were any immediate threat to you or me. I'll trust you on that point. For the moment, I'm going to assume you're psychic and know that to be true." When he didn't rise to the bait, she gave another small smile. He couldn't help feeling she was enjoying this.

"It looks to me as if someone shot at you. Judging by the track mark in the wood and a couple of fresh holes behind you, that seems to be more than a probable scenario. I'm thinking very likely. You also have some bloody spots on your face. Splinters from the ricochet perhaps?" She paused a moment. "No comment? Okay, fine. The woods across the inlet would be a good spot for

a shooter, don't you agree? And it wouldn't be too diffi-
cult a shot."

He was starting to feel like the boys at the Alamo. He
didn't know if she was a good sheriff but there was
nothing wrong with her mind. He tried to defuse the
coming explosion. "Alleged shooter, but it's your story.
Maybe we can make it into a movie of the week."

She pinned him with her gaze. "You have a new
weapon that you seem very eager to get rid of. I'm going
to take another little psychic leap and assume it's the
alleged shooter's weapon and that you don't know their
identity. I'm also guessing, and I'm pretty sure of this
one, any self-respecting shooter would never give up their
gun on purpose. And I can't imagine that type of person
would run away and drop their weapon—even if they
saw...what was it? A bear or big cat. So, should I wonder
if there's a body somewhere? Or bodies?"

Her voice went low and rumbled like coming thunder. "The reason I'm asking all these boring questions is
because we have this big-assed bass tournament going on
with about a hundred people on the lake, not counting
looky-loos and normal boating traffic. I don't want
anyone to snag something big out in the water that's
going to ruin his or her day and result in somebody's
YouTube upload with a million views going viral and
Twitter going wild with a hashtag of *#LookWhatIFound*.
The Chamber of Commerce wouldn't like that kind of
publicity. Neither would I." Her stare didn't flinch from
his gaze.

Jim was having trouble battling her gaze and impec-
cable logic. He couldn't remember anyone staring at him
with such intensity and longevity. Ever. "I wouldn't know
anything about alleged bodies. Or care to." Pausing for a

moment, he decided to calm her fear. "Although I'm guessing, and this is all hypothetical, nothing will turn up to embarrass anyone. And in particular...law enforcement."

Her body language relaxed a bit as she snorted back a laugh. "Well, thank God for that."

She sighed, dragging it out for a long moment. "You know you're pushing it here. That kind of story would have a normal person in interrogation for hours, maybe even lock up. I can't help but think you have little respect for me or my badge because I'm fairly certain you wouldn't have tried to pull this on Johnny."

Now he wished he'd come clean from the start. He never liked lies. "That's not true, Rita. I have nothing but deep respect for you as a law officer and as a friend."

He watched her turning that over in her mind. "Then talk to me as a friend."

It was hard not to tell the truth, but he felt it would put a strain on her sense of duty. And he still had his reasons, bad as they were. When he didn't reply right away, Rita pinched two fingers above her nose, squeezing her eyes shut for a moment.

Her sigh was long and drawn out. "I suppose you'd like to know who this gun belongs to, and think there are prints on it?"

He watched her eyes. He'd heard once that people with the same eye color seemed to be able to read each other better and form a connection. His answer came out before his mind could filter his response.

"Maybe I'd like to return the gun to its rightful owner. Personally."

His words made her flinch and then shiver. "That

doesn't seem smart, Jim. Do you have enemies, anyone who might want you dead? Can you think of anyone?"

He'd traveled that road in his mind. It was dusty and circular. "Maybe a couple of pissed off warlords in Afghanistan." His voice faltered a bit, as a stray, unwanted thought occurred to him. He shook his head, as if he'd bitten into something sour.

She stepped over and put her hand on his shoulder. "What? What is it?"

"Alina." He said the word as if he'd smelled a fish three days dead, because that's how he felt.

"Alina? Your Russian girlfriend? I heard a couple of weeks ago that you broke it off with her. You think she's involved? Was she *that* pissed off?"

Her knowledge of his love life both startled and embarrassed him. Did everyone know his personal business? How did she know that? He'd been living the life of a hermit since then, licking his wounds and waiting for law enforcement to show up.

"I haven't mentioned that to anyone."

She smirked at him, a look he guessed she must reserve for small children touring the jail.

"You're kidding me, right? I'd guess you don't know Agnes very well. Limestone is a small county and I'm sure she has her own fleet of spy drones and is on speed dial with every prosecutor in the state. Besides, I knew it before she did. So, spill. All of it."

The anger came bubbling to the surface again. "Well, let's just say a couple of weeks ago I canceled Alina's membership in Club Lane on the Lake."

He glanced at her, anger surfacing just from the memory, before re-setting the cap on his head.

"There may have been injuries involved."

SIX

RITA COULDN'T SPEAK for a moment. She wasn't surprised at a woman being hit—it happened with all too frequent regularity. The surprise was that Jim would do it.

"You hit her? Really?"

That was something she'd never dreamed he would do, or could do. Johnny hated men who beat on women and would never have had respect for Jim if he were one. As she watched, emotion played across his face, from apparent anger to a slight smirk of...what? Satisfaction? There may be depths to this soft-spoken man that no one really knew, and that made the butterflies start tickling her stomach again.

It was a full minute before Jim responded. "Well, it wasn't direct contact. It was more of a collateral nature."

She shook her head, trying to visualize how a person indirectly hit someone. Time for a different tact. Maybe playing buddies would work. She needed to take things down a notch. "Got any more beer in your fridge?"

He nodded.

"Let's get in out of this drizzle. I have a feeling the next part of this story is going to be good."

"Aren't you on duty or something?"

She noticed his gaze fall to her chest. Again.

"Nope." Then she smiled, turning his words on him. "Well, not directly."

She brushed past him and walked into the cabin. All the permutations of the situation rattled around in her head and she couldn't seem to find a good one to settle on. Considering this new information, she wondered if she could resign her commission now.

"And there's a damned good chance I'll never be on duty again."

His eyebrows shot up. "Why would that be?"

He turned to follow and she knew he was watching her walk. A girl always knows.

"Why wouldn't you go back to duty?" he asked again.

Why indeed? She wondered if they'd get to the discussion of friendship versus duty. When she stopped, he almost collided with her.

"Right now," she continued, "I'm on vacation. I know that's kind of a gray area. In a strict sense, law enforcement is never off duty, but we'll go with that anyway. And it's a good thing. If I were officially on duty, given what I suspect right now, I'd have to take you in for questioning—maybe water board you, or even worse, sic Agnes on you."

He smiled at her. "All you have is a splinter on a porch rail and a couple of holes in the wall, possibly made by wood-boring bees. Not much of a crime scene."

His voice was calm and nonchalant as he kept walking toward the kitchen. "I have an awful time with those bees."

She played along, diverting toward the leather couch. "And there's a nice sniper rifle, don't forget that."

"Scoped and suppressed does not make it a sniper rifle. It could belong to a shy and discreet hunter who doesn't like attention." He reappeared with a couple of beers and handed her one. "So, is this interrogation what I get for being such a good citizen and trying to return something I found to its rightful owner?"

He settled on the other end of the couch and she raised her bottle in salute. "Allegedly found, didn't you say? So, let's get to the good parts. Tell me about Alina's fall from grace and how she may have been...sort of injured."

———

LOOKING AT RITA, it struck him how the two women were complete opposites. Alina was an actress, well maybe—blonde hair and blue eyes with flawless skin and a slim body. In her younger days, she'd been a model. Or so she said.

Now, he knew how good an actress she was and had a deep suspicion about the type of modeling she did. He knew why he'd always had a distrust of actors. How do you know when they are acting? He'd never be able to trust her.

Rita, on the other hand, had black hair to go with her deep-blue eyes, her skin tones were dusky and glowed with health. Tiny crow's feet graced her eyes when she smiled, complementing her beauty, but were something Alina would never allow to mar her face.

There was no doubt in his mind Rita could easily move in the same fashion circles as Alina. She was beautiful enough but her beauty was deep, not the shallow version Alina sported. He doubted Rita could stand that lifestyle anyway. From what he'd seen and heard, she was all up front and seemed to carry her heart on her sleeve. There weren't any hidden agendas.

He quickly relayed the short version of the story. In fact, it even surprised him how little there was to tell. He met Alina a year ago when the party boat she was on broke down in the middle of the lake. The revelers managed to call the water patrol. Since they couldn't get there within a few minutes, Johnny Morris called Jim to see if he could help.

Jim motored his boat to theirs, tied it off, and boarded the pontoon boat. He threw out a couple of anchors the would-be sailors were too drunk to know about. They were in shallow water, so weren't in any danger unless it was from drowning. After securing their position, he had to stay to make sure no one fell off the boat.

Rita stifled a yawn indicating her obvious excitement to the story. "If this were a book, I'd have put it down already. Let's cut to the chase. How did you and Alina become an item?"

"It was pretty simple on her part, and I suppose clueless on mine. She was the only sober person on the boat. When she asked if I'd give her a ride back to the marina so she could pick up her car, I agreed."

He looked at her with an embarrassed shake of his head. "I didn't look at it as a big deal. To be honest, she was beautiful and dressed in three tiny strips of cloth she called a bikini. You might say I'd been out in the woods too long. One thing led to another and she didn't leave the cabin for the rest of the weekend. We were together from then on. After a few months, she made it plain that we should be exclusive and I agreed. Looking back, I guess she meant I should be."

The last comment suddenly riveted Rita's attention. "Doesn't sound like much of a concession on your part since you weren't exactly dating others anyway. I take it you didn't want to marry her?"

He could feel the anger boiling up again and pushed it down. "Nope. I thought about it, but she would've been a weekend wife. During the week, she kept a hotel room in Branson to be close to her work. She came to the lake on weekends or the occasions she had time away from her stage career."

Rita chuckled. "Gee, how could that ever be a problem?"

He frowned at her sarcasm.

"So." She smirked at him. "Trouble in paradise started...how?"

"Well, she started rehearsing for a new show and even started missing weekends. She said it was at a more adult-oriented theater. I didn't like that because she said it would include full nudity. Of course, when I objected, she pointed out it wasn't much worse than her little thong outfit she called a bikini.

"I've been all over the world and I'm not a prude. Still, there seemed to be something off about the whole thing and I told her so. It was hard to believe any place in Branson would have a show like that, since they advertise being family oriented.

"Anyway, she called me every name she could think of in Russian and English. I added a few more hillbilly verses just to help her vocabulary. She left in a huff and went back to her hotel."

His bottle was empty and he didn't continue until he'd returned with fresh drinks for both.

"By that evening I'd convinced myself the nudity thing was part of show biz, although I didn't like it and I'm not the sharing type. I felt crappy about the fight we had and somehow decided I'd been unreasonable, so I hopped in the truck and headed for Branson."

"It was late evening when I arrived. I got to her hotel, took the elevator, and came out on her floor. A young woman with a clipboard stopped me. It seemed the theater company leased the whole floor. She checked her clipboard after I gave her my name and said I wasn't on the list and had no business there."

He paused, shaking his head. "That pissed me off, so I tried again. I told her I was there to see Alina Ivanov."

The girl just shook her head, chewing gum like a bored teenager. "Sorry. She and Tony are rehearsing in her room. It's a closed rehearsal and they can't be disturbed."

"I just looked at her. This preppy little gal was not helping my mood at all."

"Wasn't it kind of late on a Sunday for a rehearsal?" Rita's voice was soft.

"That's what I thought. So, I walked past the girl, found Alina's room and barged right in. They didn't lock the door. With the head of steam I had, it wouldn't have mattered. The bedroom door was open, too. Anyway, the assistant was yelling and pulling at my shirt as I went in. I think she was making a lot of noise to warn them."

He shook his head. "It was a wasted effort. You might say he was deep into rehearsal, and they had their parts down good and loud."

Rita took a long drink from her beer bottle, stifled a

belch with a giggle. "So, you caught her in bed with this Tony guy?"

He nodded, still not being able to rid himself of the visual. "I'm thinking he was her leading man during the week. I was just a weekender."

She was shaking her head, but a small smile graced her face. "Wow, that's just...wrong. And ugly."

He gave a sigh and looked at the floor. It wasn't one of his proudest moments. "To be honest, I may have gone a little overboard."

Sympathy showed in her expression as she nodded. "I can understand that." Her expression sharpened. "Maybe you'd better define...a little overboard."

He looked at her and then shook his head, not meeting her eyes. "He was working hard on his part."

She rolled her eyes.

"They were so engrossed with each other they didn't see me, or even hear the assistant yelling at me."

"And...? C'mon, Jim. You're killing me here."

"I may have kicked him in the balls."

Her hand was covering her mouth. He couldn't tell if she was trying not to laugh or was shocked. He could see her eyes filling with tears, so shocked was out.

"So, then you hit her?" she squeaked out.

He shook his head again. "I said I didn't hit her. He was standing at the end of the bed, while..."

She waved her hand at him. "Yeah, yeah. I got it."

"Anyway, I kicked this Tony hard enough that he lunged over her and went face first into the headboard."

When he was silent for a time, she prompted him again. "And...?"

"I guess they were still connected, so to speak, when he went flying over her. I may have helped him with another kick or two. When I left, they were both rolling around and screaming."

She sat with her mouth open, slowly shaking her head. It took another long pull on the beer bottle before she started laughing. He couldn't help joining her when she snorted beer through her nose, which brought on another giggling fit. When she gained control of herself, she wiped her face with the palm of her hand.

"Damn. I'd like to have seen that."

"Yeah, well. I guess I should have sold tickets. On the way out, I asked the assistant if they rehearsed like this often. After she found her voice, she replied they did it most every day."

He stared at the floor. "Talk about clueless. Anyway, at that point I told the assistant to tell Alina not to come back, and I went home. I boxed up all her crap and shipped it to her. That was a couple of weeks ago. Since I didn't hear from anyone, I guess no charges were filed. We weren't married, so no harm, no foul, I suppose. Life goes on."

They were both silent for a few moments. Her gaze was on him long enough that he started to feel uneasy.

Her voice was soft when she spoke. "It's never no harm, no foul. Do you love her?"

It was about time for an easy question. "You know, I've thought a lot about that. I think it was more...that I wanted to. I guess the family clock was ticking and I was lonely. Maybe I was impatient for something close to a normal home. But thinking about it, we never had much in common to talk about. After what I saw in that hotel room, she's yesterday's news. And that doesn't bother me at all."

"You sure?"

He'd thought a lot about that too. "Well, I've read there's a fine line between love and hate. I think the true sense of it is indifference. I don't think I ever loved her. Right now, I'm kind of relieved I don't have to deal with her."

Rita nodded and seemed to come to a decision. "Do you think she'd be mad enough to try and kill you? You had to mean more to her than a bass boat and cabin by the lake. She did make the effort to come and see you often, I guess. Why would she do that?"

He thought it over a moment, which forced him to remember the times he and Alina had been together. It'd been like a honeymoon every weekend. They didn't go out much at all. He remembered wondering about that several times. She seemed content to stay in the cabin or go boating.

"No, I don't think she would want me dead or injured. But then, I never thought she'd do what she did, so who in the hell knows? As for making the effort to see me? Maybe this was just an escape from her reality and I was the rent she had to pay."

"I think you're right about that." She lined up her empty bottle next to the other one on the end table. "You got anything to drink with a little more kick to it?"

He retrieved a bottle of Jack Daniels from a cupboard in the kitchen and poured her a water glass half full. She drained it and asked for another. He couldn't figure out what she was doing. Was he being clueless again? His female read-o-meter was clearly broken. "Are you sure about this? You might want to slow down."

She gave him a crooked smile. "Figuring out all your problems is going to take a lot more than beer."

"Okay, but this stuff can sneak up on you." He could

tell she wasn't a big drinker as indicated by her words that already slurred a bit. Then she started to talk. It was as if she needed the alcohol to let the floodgates open.

"Did you ever lose anyone you loved beyond all reason? And I don't mean the Russian. That doesn't count." She paused and looked at him with bleary eyes. It was the quickest drunk he'd ever seen. "I think there was an office pool several places giving odds for when things would blow up between you two. That was a no-brainer. Everyone could tell you weren't thinking with your big head on that one. So, anyone at all, Jim?"

He started to answer but she talked over his response.

"Johnny and I went way back. We were both military police. We'd enlisted right out of high school. God, you know everything at that age. We met at our first duty station. Hit it right off and were never apart after that." She paused to take another drink, but part of it spilled on her blouse.

Jim settled back into the cushions, wondering where this was going.

Rita's unfocused gaze was somewhere across the room, or someplace he wasn't allowed to see. "We got out of the service after twenty years, took our retirement and came home. Then he ran for sheriff. As soon as he won that election, he made me his chief deputy. I had more experience than all the other deputies combined. Some of them didn't like that and I had to give out a couple of attitude adjustments. After that, things ran smooth. Johnny and I made such a great team."

She stared off into space, seeing things he could never fathom. It seemed as if she took each memory and examined it, looking at all the cracks and blemishes that come with age.

"You remember what happened?" Her voice was strained. "Dammit, he wasn't supposed to be there. The sheriff's job is paperwork and administration. You don't pull patrol duty. I was on the other side of the county serving a summons at the time and didn't know he was out and about. By the time I was called, it was too late. Damn him for being so careless. How could he do that to us?"

Her anger made her sound almost sober. He could remember so many times in his life he'd seen comrades fall, but none of those experiences seemed to apply. "I'm sure he was doing his job the best he knew how. It was bad luck."

"Yeah, bad luck. That's what everyone tells me." Her voice was low enough he strained to hear. "I never got to say goodbye. One day he's there and the next...I still miss him so much. It never goes away. The way he touched me, loved me...made me laugh when I needed it." She shrugged and shook her head. "Agnes says I need to get out more...to let him go. How do I do that?"

She'd been leaning back against the cushions, and then sat upright, running a hand through her hair. Somewhere in the conversation, her ponytail came undone. Thinking she was about to fall off the couch, he came over to her. She grabbed him around the neck and tried to kiss him, her lips leaving a sloppy trail across his cheek.

"Whoa, where did that come from?" He chuckled, wishing she were sober. As she'd pointed out, Alina hadn't been around all that much lately and Rita was a beautiful woman. "How about we put this off for a while? At least, until you can remember it."

Her voice faded as her clutching fingers relaxed. "It's been so long…"

He laid her back on the couch and stretched her out. After placing a throw pillow under her head, he took off her boots and loosened her belt after taking off the Glock in a clip-holster. He liked her choice in everyday carry—same as his. Her cell phone fell from her blouse pocket, so he grabbed that. He found a snub-nosed .38 revolver tucked in the small of her back, along with a knife in her boot—and a wicked little tool it was. He put everything on the end table, easy to find, and then covered her with a patchwork quilt that he kept draped over the back of the couch.

He made sure the trash can he put by her head had a disposable bag in it. Having done all he could do, he went back out on the deck to commune with the cacophony of crickets and tree frogs.

SEVEN

HE RETRIEVED Rita's cell phone, searched through her contacts for the correct number, and called Agnes on her personal cell number to let her know where one of her chicks was for the night. He didn't know the dispatcher well, but knew enough to know she took her job seriously.

"Is she drunk?" The woman's voice was resigned. Her voice made him think of better times and fun places.

He laughed. "Plastered. It only took a couple of beers and a JD. She's not much of a drinker."

"Hey, that's a good thing." She paused a moment and he waited her out.

"She just can't let Johnny go and she's so lonely she doesn't know what to do with herself. There was an incident today and it brought all the bad memories back. She's vulnerable right now. Maybe more than usual."

"It'll take time, I guess. We all have our ghosts." He was thinking a little time wouldn't hurt him either. Too much was happening and way too fast.

"She'll be fine here." He continued. "My couch looks a lot better with her on it."

The sexy voice turned sharp. "Jim, don't you dare…"

"Hey, pull in your horns. She's a grown woman." He tried to make his voice aggrieved but couldn't do it, even though he felt irritated. And he couldn't blame the woman for being protective. "It never crossed my mind, Agnes. I don't bother drunk women. If I was that kind, it would already be a done deal. Your sheriff is in less than pristine condition but her virtue is secure. Y'all have a good evening, ya hear?"

"Wait." He heard her sigh over the phone. "Look, I'm sorry. Maybe she has lost her way for a while, but she needs an anchor. She's a damned good woman and needs the right man to help put those ghosts you mentioned to rest."

His breath came out in a long sigh. With a cold knot in his belly, and his mind wishing for things he couldn't have, he listened to the wind in the trees and Boney's leg thumping on the deck as he scratched.

Their conversation reminded him of late-night talk radio with people calling in with their woes of love—first time caller, long time listener.

Here's a dedication…

"There is only one problem with that, Agnes."

"And…?" she prodded when he was silent.

"I'm not a good man."

———

JIM RELAXED in his deck chair. Nighthawks and swallows worked the surface of the lake. There was no shortage of mosquitoes for them. The birds flew high and then swooped down toward the surface. Getting their fill of flying insects, they glided just above the surface, dipping their bill to get a drink. It was quite an aerial show. He'd heard of big bass meeting them at the surface but figured that didn't happen often. More likely it would be a sparrow hawk or prairie falcon busting them in mid-air, leaving a cloud of feathers drifting in a near-weight-less dance toward the water.

When the sun went down, bats would take over the feast. With no moon, it would soon be dark as the bottom of a well. Night would close in like a blanket. Oppressive to some, comforting to others, but never ignored.

His thoughts turned to the shooter. The biggest question was who sent him? How long before someone missed him? Who watched for news of his death? Will they send someone else to finish the job? The sniper looked to be at least a semi-pro. He couldn't imagine him being there without support of some kind, so he was certain someone was monitoring...somewhere. And back to the big questions. Who? Why?

One name kept cropping up as the source of all this. The one piece of the puzzle that didn't fit. Alina. Jim couldn't get his mind around that. What had he missed in her personality? Could she do something like this, and even more important, would she?

When it was complete dark and the mosquitoes came out in full force, he went back inside and checked to see if Rita was still comfortable. She'd turned onto her side and snored softly. Her breath blew tendrils of her hair. With a gentle touch so as not to wake her, he brushed it away from her face. It startled him to see her smile in her sleep.

To say he wasn't interested in her would be a lie. But she seemed to have more baggage than he did, if that was even possible, and baggage always made things awkward. They both were haunted with bad memories. She was struggling to find the right road out. He was just struggling.

Satisfied she was all right, he turned on the light in the restroom so she could find it if she woke in the middle of the night, secured the rest of the house, and went to his bedroom. Undressing, he placed his gun on the nightstand. It was temporary. When he turned the lights off, the gun would go under his pillow. Old habits die hard.

He picked up a western novel from the same night-stand and sat on the edge of the bed, staring out the window toward a lake he couldn't see.

He'd killed a man today and wasn't sorry. It wasn't his first. He was no virgin at that. He hoped it would never happen again, but didn't have many expectations of that. The man had his chance to give it up and live, but it didn't work out that way. He never set out to kill some-one. There were exceptions, but they were rare.

The death of the shooter gave no answers. It only left questions and possibilities. Maybe the man died because Jim was getting older, and slower—his reaction time was off. Maybe he could have shot to wound and at least gotten some answers to the questions that now swirled through his mind. Or maybe wounding the guy would have just given the shooter another chance at Jim. The situation was full of maybes and could have beens.

Deep down, he knew all those assumptions were untrue. There simply wasn't time. The shooter signed his own death warrant by being too quick. He felt no remorse for the killing. And that bothered him too.

A Louis L'Amour novel might give him some insight into that. Or not. But it wouldn't hurt to try. There was a lot of truth in the western genre, where motives were laid bare and solutions were simple and straightforward.

EIGHT

ALINA IVANOV surreptitiously watched the activity in the room from the single recliner furnished by Skaggs Hospital in Branson, Missouri, as she pretended to read a magazine. If she were casting characters for a gangster movie, she couldn't have done better than the players before her.

She couldn't count the times she regretted her dishonesty with Jim Lane. In more ways than anyone could fathom. But it was too late. That proverbial ship had sailed with an angry hurricane of wind filling the main sails and following seas to ease the journey. Trying to not think about it didn't help. It was like telling someone not to think about the giraffe peeking in the window wearing a red bow tie and purple hat. Useless.

Two days ago, Tony Kumarin gave up and agreed to surgery for the removal of one of his testicles. He was not happy, even when she told him they were both lucky to be alive. It had been a long two weeks since Jim caught her in bed with Tony. She'd tried to reach out, his anger hurting her more than she expected. But she knew him, had studied him, and with that knowledge, knew the calls were useless. At least for now.

And the last place she wanted to be was here, babysitting an idiot. But she'd been informed family was family and until otherwise informed—she had the job.

She glanced at her phone to check messages and then sighed. Not a word from him. How could she make him understand? The little voice in her head responded—you can't...you won't...not a chance in hell. There were too many things he didn't know about her, about family. Things she was unwilling to share—couldn't share on penalty of her life. They weren't a big family, nothing like the big Mafiosos, but they held a certain amount of territory and influence—even while keeping things low key and relatively out of sight.

"So, Gregory." Her attention sharpened as Tony quizzed the man standing at the foot of his bed. "What news do you have for me?"

Gregory Kumarin didn't meet Tony's gaze, instead choosing to alternate between looking at the floor and ceiling, or at Alina's legs. She admired his act, thinking he was a better actor than her, and uncrossed her legs to torment him. His gaze didn't miss a thing, and she caught a fleeting smile. Well, more of a tick on the corner of his lips. The man didn't know how to smile. He wore a rumpled gray suit with no tie and held a matching felt hat. In the nervousness he worked to project, he'd crumpled and about torn the hat brim away. She knew it was a cheap prop. Gregory Kumarin was a longtime soldier working for her father. He was loyal to one person and one person only. Even though they were cousins, that person was not Tony Kumarin—never would be. It was her father, Anton Ivanov.

"Gregory." Tony's voice was sharp with frustration, trying to get the man's attention.

"Okay." Gregory seemed to marshal the nerve to speak, although when he turned his head, he winked at Alina. He'd been glancing around the room, and Alina knew he was looking for possible sources of cameras and microphones.

Finally, he shrugged. "Since our usual contractor was unavailable, we hired some people and then they sent a man to find this Lane guy. So far, our man ain't come back. I think there's a good chance he got disappeared."

She couldn't stop her sharp intake of breath before interrupting. "Wait. What? My god. Tony—Gregory, what have you done?"

Tony glanced her way. "Shut up, Alina. You got no say in this. I'm lying in this bed mainlining painkillers and wondering where my nut went. This is all your fault. You should have kept your man happy and out of our business. If you'd done that, he wouldn't have come looking for you and busted into our room."

She couldn't believe her ears. "You damned coward! You don't kill a man because he kicks your ass."

"Oh, yeah. Sure. Only if you're ordered to. Right, Alina? Don't pull that righteous act with me. I know what you do."

After a brief stare-down, Tony's attention switched back to Gregory. "So, what's going on now?"

Gregory watched the byplay with interest as he continued. "The operator that was sent in was supposed to be good and came well recommended. Now the controller on the ground can't find him. The operator vanished. No check-in. No nothing. We know he didn't drive out because a sheriff's deputy ran a make on his vehicle and impounded it. They're waiting for someone to claim it. It will show as stolen, so we got no worries, but it's still a complication we don't need."

He shot a look at Alina. "We should have had more information before we started. My guess is Alina didn't tell us everything about Lane. Maybe some real important stuff."

Alina unflinchingly met his gaze. "I didn't tell you anything at all, because it was none of your business. It shouldn't be now."

She turned her gaze to Gregory. "If you'd bothered to ask, I'd have told you to abort this fiasco." Her voice held a menace that made him step back. She might just be a worker-bee in the grand scheme of things, but she was still the daughter of his boss.

Tony snorted and then winced. "So, big deal. We underestimated this man. We'll change tactics a little and send someone different. My people came up with just the one. He likes things up close and personal, if you know what I mean. Freddie the Shank just got out of prison and is looking for work. He wants a stake to go to Florida and get a suntan, that prison pallor doesn't suit him. The Shank won't miss." He shifted in the bed, easing the pain a little. "Who is the handler?"

Gregory was staring at the floor again. "I reached out to your cousin Viktor. Knowing how crazy he can get, he was the last choice, but everyone else was busy."

"Shit!" Tony rolled his eyes at the ceiling. "That's the old man's personal soldier. The guy is old school with a serious screw loose. If Anton hears of this, he'll feed my other ball to the dogs. Don't screw this up, man. If I go down, we all go down."

"We'll get it done," Gregory stated mildly while staring at the man on the bed a moment and then turned to leave. Alina knew his subservience was an act. The parting look he gave Tony would make most men pee their pants, but Tony always assumed he was untouchable.

"One more thing." Gregory paused at the door. "You're family, so we'll take care of this for you. I'll call you when it's over. Just so you know—your favors are all used up with this. Any more fallout will land on your head." He nodded once to Alina and left.

She walked to the bed. "Tony, don't be a fool. Give up this revenge. If Pop hears you've used one of his trusted soldiers for this, without his consent, he could kill us both. This is just the type of publicity we're trying to avoid."

Pacing the room ended abruptly; there just wasn't room. "Jim didn't understand the situation and now he won't talk to me so I can explain. I never thought he'd find out. It was a mistake on my part, but don't make it worse than it is. You and I have equal standing in this organization. I'm asking you to stop. This will get out of control."

He stared at her as he fished for the television remote trapped under his blanket. "You have feelings for Lane?"

She didn't drop her gaze. "Of course I do. I lived with him off and on for a year. He's a good man and doesn't deserve this."

"I didn't deserve this either." Tony reached out and grabbed her arm, twisting until she grimaced in pain. "You'd better order your black veil. He's history, and I don't care if you like him or not. Nobody does this to me without paying the price. And don't you try to warn him. We're related, somewhere back down the line. The organization is family. You can't go against your own flesh and blood. You know that."

Alina wrenched her arm free. "You idiot. Thanks to you, he's already been warned. You damned fool. Not only did your first attempt miss, but the odds are every single person you send in after him will disappear too. You don't understand what you've done. Call this off before you get us all killed."

Tony used the remote to lower the head of the hospital bed before he replied. "Be careful you don't have an accident of your own, Alina. Now get the hell out of here and leave me alone."

She marched from the room, then stood outside the door trying to control her breathing. Gregory was waiting for her at the end of the hall.

"How'd you get tied up with that sleazeball, Alina? This'll kill your father. You know he's looking for you to take over when he's gone."

"Yeah, like I'd ever want that job." She ran her fingers through her hair before squaring her shoulders. "There have been a few occasions that I've let people off the hook if they promised to disappear—gave a second chance. Somehow Tony found out about a few of them. Blackmail is the second oldest sin, right behind prostitution. Now I'm guilty of both. I probably deserve whatever I get."

Gregory contemplated her a moment, shaking his head slowly. "We'll see, Alina. Things ain't always as bad as they look."

Watching him walk away, she took a shuddering

breath. They didn't know what was in store for them. Even she wasn't completely sure. But she'd seen the scars, saw how his eyes never stopped checking his surroundings, heard his rambling and disjointed talk while he slept—knew a warrior when she saw one. This madness had to stop, but Tony was serious and she knew he would not. She knew of Ivanov women who died for interfering with their male counterparts. But then if she did nothing, they might both end up dead anyway. Damned if you do and damned if you don't.

Exiting the hospital, she took out her cell phone. She hadn't talked to her father in a long time and didn't know if he'd even take her call. This was not the usual mode of operation and he didn't like change. Their normal communication was a cryptic text, usually just a name and date the assignment needed to be completed. Her usefulness to the family was steeped in secrecy and she'd done her best to maintain that. Rumors that her father had mellowed drifted around, but that was intentional. She knew better. The family, under his direction, took precautions to stay under the radar. This problem and Tony's solution would not fit that scenario. The head of their family would not be pleased, and it was time to save herself. To hell with Tony. She'd just have to roll the dice.

She suspected it would be an impossible task to convince Jim her indiscretion didn't mean anything. How do you tell someone that Ivanov women used sex as a tool to accomplish a goal like a farmer would use a tractor and plow? She was raised that way, all of them were. Jim's reasoning would be wrapped in morality— something she understood as an abstract.

She keyed numbers on the secure cell phone and held it to her ear. Her other hand pressed her nauseated stomach as her nerves jangled. Sitting on a concrete bench, well away from prying ears, she was afraid the conversation she was about to have would drastically affect her life—and not for the better. For the first time in her life, she thought of disappearing.

NINE

JIM WAS SIPPING his second cup of coffee when he heard Rita moan. He took a fresh cup of brew and four ibuprofen tablets from the counter and strolled into the living room. She was sitting up on the couch with embarrassed bewilderment painting her face. As he watched, she turned white as a sheet and her hand gripped her stomach, seeming to fight down nausea by sheer will.

Taking the cup, she washed down the pills and gave him a soft thank you. He watched her shudder and could see it was a lost cause. As she abruptly came to a wobbly stance, one hand out for balance, he pointed toward the hall. She walked gingerly to the bathroom, stood still a moment, and then worshipped the porcelain throne of hangovers for a few minutes.

When it sounded like the crisis was over, he moved down the hall. "New toothbrushes are in the drawer by the sink." He shook his head and returned to the kitchen to make toast and get more ibuprofen.

After her bout in the bathroom, Rita staggered toward him. Her face had regained some color. She took a piece of toast from his plate and took a bite. Pausing a moment to shudder again, she swallowed and then took another.

Finally, she found her voice. "Well, that's an adventure I don't want to repeat anytime soon. Or, ever. How much did I drink last night?"

His voice was skeptical as he watched her eat. "Better slow down on that. You tied one on pretty good."

"Yeah, I did. That's not like me. I'm kind of a lightweight in the drinking department." She held his gaze. "Thanks for last night. I kinda remember offering myself up, maybe?"

At his nod, she continued. "So, thanks. You know, for not...I mean, for not...we didn't, I know. But...thanks."

"Kind of a lightweight?" He chuckled. "You had two beers and a whiskey."

He held up his hand at her panicked expression. "Nothing inappropriate happened. Not my style. But don't trust me to pass up the offer twice, though. You're a beautiful woman."

When she started to answer him, her phone chirped some distance away. She raised her eyebrows at him when she saw it on the end table. Balancing her way to the phone, he could see she was trying to keep her head from moving.

"Hey, Agnes. Wassup. Crap. My phone's dying. I'll call you back."

She walked back to the kitchen and held out her hand. With an exaggerated sigh, he handed her his cell phone. A moment later, she connected with Agnes again.

Her face glowed red as she talked, and judging from what little he heard, he could only imagine the interrogation she was getting from Agnes.

"Yes, I am. Uh, no. NO. Dammit, I'm pushing forty

for God's sake. Gimme a break. Yeah, I'll fill you in later. Is that the reason you called, just to give me a hard time and fuel your gossip machine? I'm on vacation, so we're not actually talking. What else do you have? Hmmm. That is strange. Okay. Look, I'll check in later and we'll go over this."

She looked at him with a small smile. "Yes, Agnes. I'll be with the hunk. For a while, anyway. Bye." She lay the phone down on the table in front of her and grabbed another piece of toast from his plate, and then watched with interest as he rummaged around in a drawer and found a charger that fit her phone.

"Alrighty then." She waved the piece of toast as she talked. "This is starting to get interesting. I want you to tell me all about your Russian friend Alina. No juicy detail is too small."

He studied her a moment before replying. This was taking a turn he wasn't comfortable with. There were a lot of juicy details. "Why? What's happened?"

She started to shake her head and stopped when her eyes lost focus. Gazing toward the bathroom, she seemed to gather herself. "We'll get to that. Now let's go back a little. You never married Alina. Why didn't you?" She sounded upbeat and friendly, but her gaze bore into him like a laser.

He tried to deflect. "Is this business or personal?"

"Maybe a little bit of both, cowboy. After all, we got drunk..."

"We?"

"...and I just spent the night at your place, with breakfast included. I'd say that puts us into good friend status, at the very least." Her fingers wiggled at him. "So, give."

"I don't remember me getting wasted." With a faint grin, he got up and popped more bread into the toaster and then broke a half-dozen eggs into a skillet. He reached into the refrigerator for hash browns, crushed bacon, and butter to mix with the scrambled eggs. It was taking him longer to gather his thoughts than it should. She was a major distraction. And looking at her smirk, she knew it.

After a couple of minutes, he replied. "It wasn't that I have some kind of psycho-babble commitment issues or anything, if that's what you're asking. I just never thought about it."

He shrugged and then grinned at her. "Alina's not the type you take home to momma."

She snorted into her coffee as she watched him stir the eggs. "Sorry. My mind's wandering. Look. Bear with me a moment. There's a reason for all this. I know you were together almost a year, but I'm curious. Out of that time, and with the schedule she apparently had, how often did she come for a booty call? Once a month? Twice?"

The question was uncomfortable only because he'd asked himself the same thing. The truth was that the whole thing was easy, too easy. And the idea that he had accepted it at face value was depressing and revealed a serious lack of smarts on his part.

He gave her an embarrassed look. "She did have a busy schedule. Sometimes she'd be here one weekend a month, sometimes less than that. She said it was more relaxing than Branson. She could just kick back and forget the world."

"So, twenty or twenty-four in-person hookups over the last year or so? Maybe less? It seems to me your hermit lifestyle suited her very well. Do you think that was by design?"

He started laughing, thinking of witness protection. "You think she was hiding out?"

She didn't laugh with him. "Well, not like you're thinking. But yeah, sort of. Think safe harbor—like disappearing. I understand you found she wasn't exclusive, but were you? I don't remember seeing you out and about with anyone local."

He realized she was getting information from him at a phenomenal rate and his voice was more defensive than he intended. "One of my problems in this modern world of ours is that I don't cheat. I'm a one-woman guy, and it seems to have worked through the years for me. When I'm with someone, I don't shop around for something else until we both call it quits. I guess that makes me a dinosaur?"

"I would consider it an asset rather than a problem, but then again, I'm not a Russian model." She thought a moment. "So, did you just assume she'd be exclusive or was it a discussion you'd had?"

"What are you, a marriage counselor?" It was Jim's turn to think a moment as he dished up the eggs and hash browns. He added a liberal splash of ketchup on his and stood open-mouthed as she asked for hot sauce. He had some Red Devil. Watching in wonder, she applied enough instant heartburn to her eggs to light up Denver.

He gave her a wary look. "I'll keep a trash can close. That's gotta come back up."

Pausing a moment, he then answered her question. "When I think about it, anytime I asked her about seeing other people, she dodged it. She always answered a question with a question. Very irritating. By the time you got through answering her questions, you wouldn't remember your own. We didn't exactly have a sit down about it, and neither of us really mentioned commitment. She talked about her lifestyle as being too hectic to settle in one place too long."

Rita nodded as she scooped eggs into her mouth between comments. "So, you were her committed and faithful anchor. Her home base so she could flit around like a butterfly and pollinate at will? She could do what she wanted and then come back home to you when she got tired of what she was doing—whatever that was— innocent or not. What a deal."

He'd already figured that out. "I never said I was smart."

"Don't feel bad about that. It's been my experience that most men aren't smart when it comes to women. And smart is the wrong word. Trusting would be better. That's why having female friends to discuss things with is important so you don't get steamrolled. What you seem to be is honest to a fault and you have that same expectation in others. That's not always practical. Just don't set the bar so high the next woman in your life can't get over it."

He raised both hands in surrender, one holding a fork. "All right, enough analysis. Why do you have this sudden interest in Alina? It's like I'm being interrogated. What's happened?"

"You're just now recognizing that? And you used to be in the security business—"

He waved the fork to interrupt. "That doesn't mean I was the guy sleuthing around figuring out who does what and why. I was more the bull in the china shop type—the Doberman, so to speak."

She nodded. "All right. That's fair. There are two reasons. The first, I will freely admit is personal. I think you're a good and decent man, which sadly there are very few of around here. I'm interested, if I didn't make that clear last night during my drunken stupor. I also figure we're both so out of practice at having an honest relationship that we should star in our own sitcom."

"You're right about that." He gave a rueful nod at that statement. "I have no idea what I'm doing."

"The second reason is more related to Occam's Razor —that the simplest explanation is usually the right one. I think your Russian love bunny is dirty. Nothing about her rings true, and if you think about it, you know it as well as I do."

"Stop." She held out her hand as a stop sign when he tried to interrupt. "You asked me to come out here. You've been dancing around the situation—the bullets, the gun—trying to keep from telling me the whole story. I don't like that, personally or officially."

He looked away. "There are reasons."

Her hand slapped the tabletop. "The hell with your reasons. You're lying by omission and making my job harder to do. Remember me saying you need a friend?"

She took a deep breath while she watched him. "But here's where it gets complicated and why I'm not taking you in on suspicion of whatever I can think up. My late husband liked you—no, trusted you. And I trusted him, simple as that. He never told me why he liked you and I never asked. Maybe it was just your boy's club keeping secrets for each other. I don't know, but he had his reasons and they were always sound."

"So it's illegal to get shot at? Allegedly?" He smiled and could tell it made her angrier. "I've given you some information, now you give some and we'll see where things go."

"Alright. I should probably have my head examined for this, but here goes. Your Alina and her family are Russian, as you know. We found an abandoned vehicle on the trail above your place that wasn't registered as being sold and had no plates. Agnes traced it by the VIN to a car lot in lower St. Louis. This car lot is a legitimate business according to our contact in St. Louis PD. However, it's also a suspected front for the Russian mob and owned by Anton Ivanov. Does that name ring a bell?"

When he shook his head, she continued. "Well it should. He has the same last name as your Russian Tinker Bell. It seems they sell cars for exorbitantly high prices, charge for work on cars that is never done, and then refund for the overcharge as a 'rebate.' It's a classic money-laundering scheme but very well structured, so St. Louis PD hasn't been able to pin anything concrete on him. I would also bet Alina's leading man is Russian. It's not much of a mental exercise from that point forward to think Alina's whole Branson career is a smoke screen. What's going on? Even for a guy that's thinking with the wrong head, it had to have crossed your mind how odd it is to have so many Russians in your playpen. What in the hell have you gotten yourself into?"

"Well, in my defense, up to now, I only knew of one. I don't have a clue what's going on...wish I did."

He met her gaze while slowly shaking his head. "All I did was kick the crap out of a man screwing my girl. Well, ex-girl. Hindsight is twenty-twenty, but I really shouldn't have done that. I knew it was over the moment I saw them. The rest was macho bullshit."

His grin grew wide. "I'd be lying if I denied some degree of satisfaction from the incident."

She started to reply but the ringing of his phone interrupted. Rita laughed. "The Darth Vader theme song from *Star Wars*?" The phone rang again and she glanced down at it, reading the caller ID. "Well, it figures." She pushed the phone across the table toward him and he couldn't read her expression. "The Dark Side is calling."

Glancing at it, he placed the phone on the table between them and put it on speaker.

"Alina."

Rita raised her eyebrows, seeming to appreciate that he included her.

"Oh god." Alina's smooth, modulated voice sounded rushed. "I'm glad you finally took my call. Baby, I'm so sorry. It wasn't what you think. I can explain everything. Please let me come home and talk to you."

"You want to come home? Are you serious? Listen to me. What you were doing was exactly what it looked like. Why you were doing it is unimportant unless it was rape, and I didn't hear any indication of that. Is the guy in jail, Alina? Did you charge him once you got free? I don't think so. Look, whatever we had together has been over for two weeks. You killed it. We're done. Finished. I'm moving on, and I suggest you do the same."

After a quick inhalation, the sound of her voice hardened. "Well, moving on may not be as easy as you think. Has anything strange happened lately?"

"You damned...!" Rita reached over and took his hand in hers, shaking her head. He took a deep breath. "What do you know, Alina? What have you done?"

"Not me, baby. If you don't believe anything else, believe this. I would never hurt you."

"Yeah, right. It's a little too late for that."

She talked through his interruption. "It was Tony. You pissed him off, and he's called in some favors."

"Favors? So, from that, I can assume he has friends in low places?" He grunted and rubbed his hand in his hair, ready to end the conversation. "I met one of his people yesterday."

Rita violently shook her head and he caught his mistake immediately. He had to find out what she knew without revealing anything unnecessary.

There was a sharp intake of breath and then a sigh on the other end of the line. "I warned them. I did, but they aren't listening. I'm so sorry. Look, I'm taking a chance here. A big one. I'm trying to fix this any way I can. Would you meet me in Springfield tomorrow? There will be someone with me. I'm hopeful we can settle this problem."

He shook his head before realizing she couldn't see it. "Can't think of a reason we should meet. I've canceled your membership at Club Lane on the Lake."

"Please, Jim. It will save lives." She sighed. "I know something of who you are...or, at least, what you are. We need to stop this now."

"And just what do you think you know about me?"

Her voice was soft. "You talk in your sleep, baby. Sometimes it scared the bejesus out of me."

Sighing, he closed his eyes a moment, feeling Rita's squeeze on his hand. His voice was brusque as he replied, "Alright. Where and when?"

"Thank you, Jim. How about the lobby of the Double-Tree Hilton? Will ten a.m. work?"

Rita nodded and he made a snap decision. "Yeah,

that'll work. I'll bring a friend with me for moral support."

The sound of sniffling came through the phone. It sounded real, but he kept reminding himself she was an actress. And in all the time he'd known her, he'd never heard her cry, so he had nothing to compare it to.

"That's all right, baby. Bring anyone you want. Do you think we can talk alone after the meeting? We really need to talk. I don't want us to end like this."

Rita was pantomiming, putting a finger down her throat and gagging with her eyes crossed. He almost laughed and felt his anger melt away, knowing she did it for a reason. Childish but effective.

"Not happening, Alina. Our days of being alone were long gone when I saw your feet waving at the ceiling."

"Please?" After a few seconds of silence, she sighed. "All right, I guess I understand. I'll see you in the morning."

He thought he heard regret in her voice but admitted to himself he was reaching. "Give your daddy my regards." He heard a definite gasp just before he severed the connection. Lost in thought, he gazed at the lake. After a few moments, he nodded and glanced at Rita. She was watching, waiting for him to say something.

When he didn't, she broke the silence. "She sounds sweet. Genuinely sorry."

"Yeah, she's a real angel. Or devil. To be honest, I've never seen them both in the same room together, so there's no way to compare."

Rita rolled her eyes at his poor joke. "So, alleged, huh? From the looks of those skid marks on the railing, you're damned lucky to be here. What were you thinking?"

She still squeezed his hand and he realized he liked it. "I'm sorry I didn't come clean. You're law enforcement, and I didn't want to put you in an untenable position. It was never a good idea, and I apologize. The cat's out of the bag now, and I think you're right. Alina must be connected big time, and I'm thinking her bed buddy is too. It sounds like that dimwit Tony reached out to some associates and they, in turn, reached out to me."

The vise-like grip left his hands. "Look, it was a mistake to tell her you met someone involved in this. Don't give up any more information. Silence is golden, especially since people have federal wiretaps on everything, including their toaster."

She gazed at him a moment before continuing. "One more thing. Anyone else would be in hiding or asking for protection. You're acting like someone just tossed a baseball through your window and you don't like it. Who are you?"

His answer was the most honest he could give. "Someone you may not want to know."

"I don't like secrets, Jim. I don't."

"Sorry, it's a long story. We can go through it when you learn to hold your liquor better." He gave her a quick grin. "But in the meantime, will you ride with me in the morning? I'd like your company and advice."

"Nope, but I'll pick you up. Your truck looks like a kidney killer."

"Your Jeep isn't much better. What if we rent something more upscale for the meeting tomorrow? Like a black Cadillac stretch limo."

"We don't have a budget for that." She came around the table and grabbed his hands. Pulling him to his feet, she planted a kiss on the corner of his mouth. "Gotta go.

See ya."

As he watched her walk away, he broke free of his surprise and caught up with her. She turned toward him with a question in her eyes, lips parted to ask a question. He thought of an old American Indian saying that spoke of kissing as breathing someone's air. Never breaking eye contact, he lowered his lips to hers. His kiss was thorough and gentle before he pulled away.

Her lips were red, wet, and open as she brought her breathing under control. He reached up and used his thumb to caress her lips with his hand holding the side of her face.

"I'm sorry. I shouldn't have done that." He watched her eyes well up with tears, and she gave a little shake of her head.

"No, it's alright. I'm just...not as ready as I thought."

"Now who's keeping secrets?" Jim took a deep, calming breath. "Look, your husband was a good man, a very good man. If you're not ready...well, that's all right. Who knows, you may never be ready for anything else. I'm not looking for a lifetime commitment at a moment's notice."

He surprised himself with a laugh that sounded more like a short bark. "I'm learning a lot about women late in my life, and I'm just slow on the uptake. Apparently, I'll make a good hermit. If you're willing, we'll take it a day at a time and you are in charge. No pressure. Agreeable?"

She gave him an unreadable look. "Thanks for understanding."

Understand? He just went from zero to sixty, then back to zero in about thirty seconds. He could blow an engine doing this.

"Oh, don't misunderstand me. I didn't say I understood, just that I'd back off. Even a dummy like me can take a hint. You were right about men never understanding women."

Her face turned a dusky red. "That's not what I...god. You're all or nothing, aren't you?"

Giving him one last glance, she paused as if she wanted to say something, and then she retreated around the corner of the veranda. Under a minute later, it sounded like her Jeep was peeling out in four-wheel drive. He didn't know they could do that.

His gaze settled on the sunlit lake, scanning the far shore for everything...and nothing.

"Shit. That went well."

TEN

THE NEXT MORNING Rita sat alone at a table in the Café. She glanced at her watch. There was an hour to kill before she needed to head for Jim's place.

What happened out there? She thought about it from the time Agnes pointed her in that direction to when she left. Everything was out of character for her. Get drunk? Pour her heart out to a stranger—well, sort of? She couldn't deny her attraction to him, but spend the night? And the big one...the kiss?

All that happened while she was trying to find out about someone taking a shot at him. What a great investigator she was. She thought about that a moment. Maybe she was like him? A bull in a china shop...or bull-ette, not a cow.

He lied to her at first, but she could understand it. If he reported the shooting, that would start a progression of events that he couldn't control. She shivered, remembering his comment on returning the rifle personally. That had retribution written all over it, something she could not allow to happen. Or shouldn't. But she did understand it.

Her mind kept coming back to the Russian woman. Could the woman orchestrate a hit? Would she carry the woman-scorned scenario that far? Maybe the tandem of Alina and Tony. No proof yet, but it sounded likely they'd done just that. Or at least had someone take a potshot at Jim. And what now? People like this didn't incriminate themselves easily. They knew how the game was played, how to stay under law enforcement radar.

The server had just brought her the special, a guaranteed heart attack egg and ham omelet with red peppers and hash browns, covered in white gravy, when she heard the familiar buzz of conversation around her come to a halt.

Glancing up, she saw a tall, white-haired man standing just inside the door. He scanned the room and as she watched, his gaze settled on her. Her eyes widened as he started toward her with a smooth, catlike grace navigating between the tables. As he got closer, she noted his clear, light-blue eyes. They were so pale they appeared white from a distance. His close-cropped hair and erect bearing screamed military to her and the clipped, precise speech put the cherry on top. Having traveled in certain parts of the world, she came to the sudden conclusion that there were way too many Russians in this playpen. Her hand rested on her weapon and when he stopped, she just knew she heard his heels click together.

"Sheriff Morris? May I sit down?"

"Free country." She indicated a chair. "What can I do for you?"

His smile was mocking.

She leaned back in her chair. This man exuded

masculinity and could sell testosterone by the gallon. She guessed his age about fifty and figured he'd escaped from the cover of a romance novel pointed toward seniors if there were such a thing. She could see him on a cover with his shirt in tatters, swooning women at his feet.

He still hadn't taken a seat. Surely not indecision? Her right hand gestured toward the empty chair across from her while her left hand pulled slightly on her sidearm. This was not starting out to be a comfortable day.

He finally sat and held out his hand. "My name is Viktor, with a K. It's nice to meet you, Sheriff Morris."

The man could easily see her hand on her pistol. To shake his hand would normally remove that threat unless she shook with her off-hand. That was a game she didn't want to play. Not running for a political office has advantages. She had no one to please but herself. When she didn't respond to his hand, he diverted it to the napkin and menu holder in the middle of the table. He took a menu but didn't look at it.

Smooth.

"You got a last name, Viktor with a K?"

He hesitated a moment. "Kumarin."

"Interesting." She stared at him. The only sounds she could hear were the rattling of dishes in the kitchen and the exhaust fan over the grill. Everyone else in the room was watching the show.

With a sudden relief, she was glad most of the people in the Café carried weapons of one sort or another. She knew a good number of them would be more than happy to step in to help if needed. They might even call it sport. Being country ain't bad. It was that kind of place.

So, let the games begin. Another Russian? Butterflies

in her stomach started a windy gale and she pushed away the heart attack special. "So, what can I do for you, Mr. Kumarin?"

"Sorry to interrupt your breakfast." The man smiled at her, but the act didn't defrost his eyes. "I'm trying to connect with a friend of mine who was taking pictures in the area. He likes to do nature photography around lakes like this one, but he seems to have disappeared."

She tried to get a read from his face, but his expression was flat as a plate. One author she'd read would describe his face as insentient as a bowl of pudding.

"You said *was* taking pictures. That's an odd choice of words. Sounds like you know something I don't. It's a real big lake. My county only covers the southern part of it. Do you have anything more specific about where this friend of yours might be?"

He stared at her a moment and then glanced at her hand resting on her pistol. "No."

As they looked at each other, she could tell this was going nowhere fast. He was fishing for information and she had a good idea of what he wanted.

"We can't do anything for twenty-four hours after you file the report," she said. "Unofficially, we can put some feelers out once we know who we're looking for."

With a quizzical look and shrug, she asked, "Does this friend of yours have a name?"

The information was slow in coming. "The same as mine, Kumarin. Dimitri Kumarin."

She never lost eye contact with the man, trying to make him nervous—and it was hard to look at those washed-out eyes. "Well, I haven't heard a thing."

Thinking of the abandoned SUV, she smiled. "Do you know what kind of vehicle he was driving?"

Kumarin was showing some situational awareness and seemed to notice the attention he was getting. Several hunters were in the room—gone were the days of safely leaving firearms in your truck. There were too many people who'd steal anything to sell for their next fix, or in some cases...groceries. A couple of rifles and several shotguns leaned against tables.

He studied the room a moment before answering. "Unknown. His family told me he hadn't checked in with them and he is very punctual about that." His eyes pinned her. "That's all I know."

Or willing to divulge? "I can understand their concern. Where, exactly, are you and your *family* from, Viktor?" She stressed the word family.

When he didn't answer, she spoke to the people around her. No one pretended they weren't listening. "Any of y'all know anything? Seen anybody, or anything, unusual? Strangers with cameras?"

That got a laugh from the crowd. "Yeah, I know." She shook her head with a smile. "Between the meth-heads and tourists, I'd have to refine that definition of unusual a little."

The man abruptly stood and looked at her. "This is a waste of my time. For a public servant, you're not being helpful. If you hear anything, we'd like to know. His family is worried."

"Could you go by the office and fill out a missing person report? It would help."

The man looked angry. Too bad.

"Got a card? Phone number? Address? How about a picture of your friend? Where may I contact you?"

"I'll find you, if needed." He moved toward the door.

What the hell was that little visit all about? He'd

walked out abruptly, like he'd said his lines and exited, job done. Rita looked at her cold omelet with distaste and jumped as Agnes slid into the chair just vacated by Kumarin.

"Oh, this seat is warm. Now, that was a handsome specimen of a man." Agnes chuckled. "Are you expanding your horizons like we talked about?"

Rita gazed at the door Kumarin had just closed, a cold knot in her belly. "That man is trouble with a capital T."

"They all are, honey. They all are." The woman paused a moment and then asked softly, "So, how did it go with Jim?"

Her fork searched the plate for something worth eating. "Ah, hell. I managed to piss him off too. I'm batting zero." Rita turned her gaze to the door. "Agnes, you watch out for that man. Put the word out to the deputies. Viktor, with a K, Kumarin. See if anything shows up on the computer. I don't like anything about him."

Her mind wandered a moment, thinking of Viktor, Alina, and Tony, an abandoned SUV and unknown shooter—although she suspected the unknown's name was Dimitri. The dots were scattered, but with just a few more and a big old lead pencil, she might just trace out a constellation. Shaking her head to clear her thoughts, she continued with Agnes.

"I'll be in Springfield the rest of the day enjoying my vacation. Let me know if anything comes up." She looked directly at Agnes. "And I mean anything. There's something brewing around here and I don't like it."

ELEVEN

JIM WAS UP BEFORE DAWN, eating a cold breakfast and watching the emerging sun burn away the fog from the shadows of the forest. He hadn't slept much the night before, jerking awake at every sound—from the cabin creaking and settling to the wind in the trees outside. To top off his insomnia, an owl decided to perch in the trees next to his window—a noisy, gregarious owl.

In the fitful attempts of sleep, the ghosts and shadows were back, dancing in his mind. In his dreams, there were enemies behind every tree—darkness, once a sanctuary, now became a hiding place for the unknown. It seemed the spirits were sending a message he wasn't ready to comprehend.

He took Boney's bowl out to the deck. The dog sidled up and Jim scratched him behind the ears a moment. "Hey, useless. You're supposed to catch your own meals, remember?"

The dog gazed at him, patiently waiting, unconcerned, certain in his partnership with this human. "Fine. Eat your breakfast. Lazy."

Once it was light enough to see and armed with his shotgun and pistol, he scouted the area surrounding his cabin. Although the area looked open, only a couple of clear lanes would allow anyone to shoot toward his house, and both were from across the water of the inlet. Unless intruders used the driveway, any other location would have trees and brush blocking a clear shot.

If they were close, he'd hear them—or the dog would. He'd have to assume long-distance shooting was their choice.

A few minutes later he stood across the snippet of lake from his cabin and near where he'd shot the sniper. He savored the early morning coolness and quiet. This was the best time of the day. The forest was still in shadow and he blended into the trees.

The dew on the grass sparkled in the morning sunlight sifting through the forest. The only tracks he saw were his own and one trail from a small animal dragging its belly—too wide for an armadillo, so a groundhog. Thinking about further attacks, he thought about making a few mantraps in the area, deadfalls or snares. But he was afraid he'd catch someone not involved with this madness, which in turn would raise questions he wasn't prepared to answer.

There weren't any close neighbors, but he still didn't want to take a chance. Although he owned his property, he was surrounded by public land and anyone could be wandering around. Being vigilant was his best bet.

When he returned to the cabin, he puttered around for a while weeding his vegetable gardens and pruning his flowerbeds. Geraniums and Gerbera Daisies always needed deadheading. He'd terraced the slope from below his back deck down to the dock and the lake with vegetable beds and flowers. The ground was so rocky the only way to grow anything besides weeds was to make a raised bed and haul in bags of potting soil to fill it. Since he'd moved into the lake home, he'd built a dozen beds.

Seeing it was still early, he gathered flat rocks and began building another terraced bed. There wasn't any lack of material to work with and he needed to stay busy. Otherwise, his mind would stay in hyper-drive pondering the what-ifs of situations he hadn't thought about...yet.

Nearing nine a.m., he went down to the pier, stripped down to his boxers, and dove into the lake to wash off the sweat and grime. Using the ladder at the end of the pier, he climbed out, gathered his clothes, and stuck his feet into his boots to navigate his way up the rocky path to the back deck.

As he started to enter his back door, he heard a noise from the end of the deck. Whirling, fumbling for his pistol, he saw Rita standing there watching him. He hadn't expected her to be early.

He clutched his clothes against his belly. "How long have you been here?"

"Oh, just long enough." Her smile grew into a full-fledged grin.

Remembering last night's conversation, he tried to bring up the anger he felt—but it was slow in coming. He stood a moment staring at her before he said in an off-hand voice, "You could turn around, you know."

She put her hand on her chest and mimicked a pitty-pat with her palm over her heart. "I don't think so. Nope. I'm good right here."

He tried to be nonchalant as he dropped the bundle of clothes into a deck chair, thinking to call her bluff and make her look away. She burst out laughing. He tried to feign anger. Another lost cause. A grin took over his face. "What the hell? This isn't my finest moment, you know. You're not doing much for my ego. Give me a break."

Her laugh was infectious and he couldn't help but smile with her. This was not working out well.

She pulled her hand from in front of her mouth and controlled her laughter. "I'm sorry, but the visual is priceless. It's the whole naked cowboy standing there in nothing but knee boots and a hat scenario. Priceless."

"I'm not naked."

"Well, you should check your wet boxers for gaps. But what the hell? We're both adults here."

He could hear her laughing again as he retreated inside the door. Once inside, he checked himself in a hall mirror. Yep. Ridiculous. So much for a good impression. He scurried around looking for semi-clean clothes.

When he came outside, he stopped and watched her. She leaned with her hands on the rail looking out at the lake. He wondered if she needed a license to wear those jeans.

"Are we in danger today?" Her voice was calm as she gazed across the inlet.

"Not unless someone sneaked in within the last few minutes." He shrugged as she turned toward him. "You never know, but I doubt it."

Once they were in the Jeep, she reduced the forty-five-minute trip to Springfield down to thirty. His grip on the padded door handle left an imprint he figured would never go away. Occasionally, she glanced over at him and laughed.

"I'm glad you find me so amusing."

"Well, it's the whole naked gardening thing. There is

an international day for that, you know. I'll have to check the calendar, but I don't think this is it."

At his chagrined look, she laughed. "Don't worry, I won't tell anyone. And I didn't get a picture, so you're safe from that." She chuckled again. "Well, I might tell Agnes. If it happens again, she will want pictures. I think she's a fan."

He gave an exasperated sigh. "You know, it doesn't help to apologize every time you laugh at me. It doesn't come through as real sincere." He knew his voice whined a little. He'd call it something more macho if he could think of the right word. Pleading? Begging?

She couldn't smother another snort. "Sorry."

"Shut up."

They whipped off I-44 onto Glenstone Avenue, blew through a yellow-lighted intersection, and turned into the parking lot of the DoubleTree Hilton two minutes later.

He thought about jumping out and kissing the ground. Before they climbed out of the Jeep, she leaned over and opened the glove box without looking inside. It looked as if she had it reinforced and made into a gun safe. She held her hand out and then sat staring at him.

When he stared back, she pointed toward the glove box. "You can't take your Glock inside, Jim. I don't think you have a concealed carry permit, and open carry might make people nervous. You know how city folk are."

"Missouri is a constitutional carry state. I don't need a permit."

She made a "gimme" gesture with her fingers. "It's also a common sense state. You need to use a little here."

He'd done the paperwork a year ago but guessed it got lost in the shuffle. Not surprising with everything that went on. "All you have to do is sign a paper, and I'd have one." He cleared the chamber, adding the ejected bullet to the magazine, and dropped both inside.

She slammed the lid closed, locking it. "I'll give it back later. I promise."

"The people we're meeting will be armed, you know." He gave her a disgruntled look as they exited her vehicle.

"And so will I." Her look was serious as her gaze sought his eyes. "This meeting is for talking only. A meeting to find out what's really going on and maybe settle differences. Got that? This won't be a shooting contest. There are too many civilians around to start anything."

Striding up the inclined parking lot, they arrived in the lobby a few minutes early and sat at one of the center fountains surrounded by padded benches. As they sat, he rubbed his arms and legs.

She reclined back against the cushions, hands folded over her belly, looking like a relaxed cat. "A little tense, are we?"

"Dammit, Rita. You couldn't have had a quarter-inch clearance between your Jeep and that tractor you passed. I'm betting the woman following with her blinkers on in the safety truck about crapped her pants. I feel like I've run a marathon."

"Just relax. Take a few deep breaths and clear your head. I know we've been trying to keep everything light, but this is dead serious. We have a chance to solve this mystery today, or with a little luck, at least put it to bed. If not, we'll have to see how it shakes out."

He followed her suggestion and after a couple of Zen moments trying to clear his head, looked over at her. "Does this mean you'll stop with the snarky little chuckles?"

She was leaning back, watching the door through slitted eyelids. "Oh, hell no. I'll try, but no promises." Snorting, she continued. "Who am I kidding? I won't ever get that visual out of my head, at least until you replace it with something better. So, why try?"

Before he could reply, she sat up. "Show time."

TWELVE

THEY WATCHED a small group of people walk through the foyer and stop at the front desk. Alina was in the group, along with a man he took to be Tony. He'd never seen the man standing up—or from the front, but he looked familiar.

Two men were with the group and his first impression was trained gorillas. They were NFL lineman huge, wearing sports jackets over turtlenecks and chinos, but moved with a light-footed grace that spoke of countless hours of training and conditioning.

She nudged him and inclined her head toward the door. Two more men, he assumed bodyguards, were standing outside. All the guards were cookie-cutter similar and they were damn big cookies.

The small group surrounded a tall, slim man dressed casually in khaki pants and a blue silk shirt. His blond hair and smooth face made it hard to judge his age. Piercing blue eyes looked neither left nor right. He led the small group toward one of the conference rooms opening into the lobby.

As they walked by, one of the mountains of flesh had a brief consult with Alina and then came toward them. When he spoke, he didn't make eye contact with either of them.

"Come with me." He then turned and walked away.

As Rita started to get up, he put a hand on her leg, pushing her back down. She looked at him in surprise and he shrugged. "I'm feeling perverse today."

That gained him an eye roll.

After the group of people entered the conference room, the bodyguards took up a position on either side of the closed doors.

Rita looked over at him and shook her head. "These guys don't get many points for smarts, do they? I wonder if they know you're missing?"

The conference room door opened. Alina came out and stared at one of the men a moment, and then moved over to them. He had to admit she had a graceful walk as she stopped in front of him.

"My father would like you to join us, Jim. That is, if you have the time? Or would you rather stay out here and play games?"

Her coolness surprised him. She was wound tight as string on a baseball. He stood and offered his arm to Rita. "Alina, I'd like you to meet my friend Rita."

"I know who she is," Alina interrupted, never taking her gaze from Jim. "It's so very nice to make your acquaintance."

"Really?" Rita seemed to be giving the other woman tight scrutiny. "You're thrilled?"

Alina glanced over her shoulder as she turned and walked away. "No."

Rita gave a little unladylike snort. "Oh, this is gonna be fun. She's so nervous I'm betting she wets herself."

"She doesn't look nervous to me." He guided her with his arm behind the small of her back and detected a slight bulge at her waistline. A hideout gun? Interesting.

She whispered, "Behave yourself. You can't let this get out of hand."

The room held a single eight-foot conference table set up in the center. When they came in, no one turned to look at them as they went around the table and sat opposite the three. Across from them, Alina was the only one standing.

Before they sat, one of the bodyguards moved toward Rita. Jim moved to intercept. "Don't even think about touching her. You've seen the badge and already know she's carrying, so there's no point."

The bodyguard stood waiting for orders, seemed to get them, and moved away. Not once did any sign of emotion show on his face.

Jim knew if he had to, he could defeat one of them, maybe both. But if more came in the door, and in a small room—all of them armed? The image of a knife fight in a phone booth came to mind.

Alina looked at him. "My, aren't we protective today? Is this my replacement?" When no one answered her, she kept her stare on Jim a moment and she turned to her right. "This is my father, Anton Ivanov." She hesitated a moment before seating herself next to her father. "You've already met Tony."

Jim smiled at the man. "How's the acting business, One-Ball?"

The mob boss lifted a hand, stopping any reply. He started in a soft voice. "Mr. Lane, I have found that if all contentious situations are handled as if they were a business deal, then any problem can be negotiated and dealt with. As you know, the *business* we have to discuss today is very private."

Ivanov's voice gave no more emotion than if he were in a boardroom. "Do you intend for the woman sitting next to you to be a part of this business?"

"The woman is Rita Morris and a trusted friend. Anything said to me can be said to her."

The man slowly inclined his head, his gaze flicking between the two of them. He reminded Jim of a snake that couldn't decide where to strike.

"Very well. It's my understanding that you caught Alina and Tony in a somewhat compromising position, and then in anger, you kicked him in the balls. After that assault, you left. Is that correct?"

"Pretty much." Jim looked at Tony. "I had to look closer than I wanted, but I did find one to kick. They were so small. The last I saw of him, he was crying like a baby and puking his guts out."

Tony was coming out of his chair when Anton spoke. "Sit down." Proving Ivanov's authority, he sat down without comment.

The mob boss steepled his fingers and looked across them at him. "Baiting Tony is not very helpful, Mr. Lane."

Jim hadn't lost eye contact with Tony. "It amuses me."

Ivanov continued. "As far as I'm concerned, the first matter is settled between the two of you. Tony transgressed against you with your woman, and you paid him back. It's over."

"Transgressed? I suppose that's a true analogy. But they were both transgressing, as you put it, and screwing like bunnies." He turned his gaze to Alina. "And as a point of order, I've come to realize she was never my woman. It seems I was a convenient diversion."

He smiled at Ivanov. "In a pure business sense, I'm glad this came to light now. It will keep further mistakes to a minimum."

After a startled gasp, Alina stared at the tabletop.

Ivanov ignored his interruption. "More important to this meeting, it came to my attention there may have been a hunting accident around your lake home, Mr. Lane. This is a regrettable incident and should never have happened." He looked at Tony until the man squirmed in his seat. "It should never have happened."

Ivanov continued. "As far as the family is concerned, this matter is closed. I'm glad you've retained your health and have no interest in how you resolved the issue. If there are additional hunters in your area, I want to assure you they won't be any concern. There shall be no more accidents."

"Just like that? With all due respect, how good is the word of a mob boss?" He didn't miss the use of the word shall instead of will. Shall is a command and promise, while the word *will* signifies an intention that leaves some wiggle room. He didn't like wiggle room.

Ivanov nodded. "Just like that. I keep my word, Mr. Lane. I'm sure you could fill a book with the names of people who doubted my word or intentions."

Jim nodded before he pointed to Tony. "When someone tries to kill me, I'm not inclined to let it go. What about him? Do you control him?"

Ivanov stared at Jim a moment and then turned to look at his subordinate. "Tony? Is there anything else about this matter to concern us—any information we don't have?"

"Boss. We'll talk later." Tony found something interesting on the desk.

Irritation was starting to show in Ivanov's voice. "This thing was started without my knowledge. You kept it from me. We'll talk about it now. I've given my word."

Jim got a bad feeling watching the byplay between the two men. It was clear Ivanov didn't expect any complications. It also seemed clear Tony wasn't too worried about the crime boss. If this were on the level, he should be. There were games afoot.

Tony was starting to squirm like a crackhead needing a fix. "There may be some players still in the field."

Alina gasped and shook her head. "Oh, no."

"Recall them." Ivanov's voice was cold as he stared at his subordinate. "They will report to me no later than this evening."

Tony's stare at Jim was malevolent. "I don't know if I can make that happen, boss. That time frame is unrealistic."

Before they could say more, the door opened and a man they'd not seen walked up to Ivanov and handed him a sheet of paper. The man left as quietly as he'd come in.

Ivanov studied the paper, forgetting Tony for a moment, and then raised his gaze to Rita.

"So, you are Rita Morris, acting sheriff of Limestone County. I knew that since you were introduced. I trust you're here alone, in an unofficial capacity?"

The guards shifted. One moved toward the door and the other directly behind her.

Rita stared back at the man, and Jim marveled at her calmness. This was one cool lady. Her voice mocked the man.

"To be clear, I'm not here in an official capacity. I can assure you there aren't any legions of alphabet agencies surrounding the hotel, unless you dragged them here as part of their major crimes surveillance. I'm just an observer and offering support to a friend—a very good friend. I'm as anxious to settle this matter as you are. Of course, you didn't introduce yourself. You and your people control most of the illegal action in the corridor between St. Louis and Chicago, correct?"

She stared unflinching at him. "And, while we're talking, is the player in the field, as Tony calls him, named Kumarin? Viktor with a K? Would he be a tall, spooky-looking man with almost white eyes? Just needs a monocle to look like a Prussian diplomat?"

Alina collapsed back into her chair. "Oh, shit."

Ivanov turned to look at Tony. "You have a lot of explaining to do. My patience with you is at an end."

The crime boss changed sheets of paper and shifted his attention to Jim. "Tell me, Mr. Lane. What is a Shepherd?"

How good was this man's information services? They would have to be very good to get any kind of sniff of his old employer. But this man had lots of money at his disposal. When the money ran out, there were always his goons to fall back on.

"Your report doesn't explain that? I'm shocked."

Ivanov almost smiled but seemed to catch himself. It left him with a grimace on his face. "Not yet. However, no records are safe, Mr. Lane. Some just require more time and money to obtain."

"Maybe he just likes sheep." Tony laughed, playing it up to the bodyguards. "You know...a shepherd?"

No one saw Jim's move in time to interfere as Tony's

face smashed down into the table and came up bloody. The conference table was made of solid wood, and it quivered from the blow. Tony held both hands to his face trying to stop the bleeding.

When the guard behind Rita grabbed for Jim, the man went reeling backward, clutching his throat. Jim glanced at Rita and her expression was calm, like this was an everyday occurrence. He saw her hand was on her pistol.

The other guard inside the room started forward and Ivanov raised his hand to stop him. The guard diverted to help his fallen comrade trying to breathe through a bruised larynx.

"Tony, if you had been raised in the Motherland, you'd know not to bait a bear when you're inside its cage." Ivanov turned his attention back to Jim. "My apologies. It's my intention that all these hostilities will cease. It attracts attention and it's not good business. Do I have your word that you'll stand down, Mr. Lane?"

He thought about it. Glancing at Rita, she shrugged, giving no advice. The last thing he needed was a war with these people. They had many resources and the will to use them. They'd grind him down with sheer numbers. It was lucky for him the last thing cockroaches want is to have light shined on them. He nodded assent.

"You have my word if I'm not provoked, this will end here. It all depends on you and if you have any control over your people. I'm concerned about your men left in the field."

"They will be recalled, Mr. Lane. Do not concern yourself with them." Ivanov made a steeple of his fingers in front of his face and peered at Jim over them. It seemed to be his habit. "You appear to be a good man. Even in my profession, I can still recognize such—

perhaps more so because of what I do. Would you consider working for me? It would be advantageous for you, and I can always use someone trustworthy."

He glanced to the side. "You could have Tony's position."

Jim looked at Alina a moment. She looked hopeful... and embarrassed.

"Mr. Ivanov, you and Alina should understand this. It's something common to all of us. The matter of infidelity is a loss of trust. She broke our contract of her own accord. There's no going back."

Ivanov glanced at his daughter. "I do understand. Trust within family is paramount. All right, then. This matter is at an end. I'm sorry, Alina. The trouble with good men is you can't buy them. As he alluded to...trust is earned." He rose abruptly and started toward the door with his entourage scrambling to follow.

Watching them walk away, Jim couldn't help feeling the whole thing was a bit too scripted, too sterile. Could they have staged this to put him at ease—one of Alina's one-act plays? It was logical for the mob boss to come and assess the threat. He'd do the same to check out competition in business. Jim wasn't sure that this entire little matter was just that—business. What else was going on?

He called to the man. "Mr. Ivanov. A moment, please." He continued when he had his attention. "If anything happens to either myself or Sheriff Morris, I'm going to hold you responsible. Have I made myself clear? Personally responsible."

"That's twice you've sought to protect the lady sheriff. You should know that makes you vulnerable." Ivanov smiled at him, shaking his head. "Mr. Lane. Accept the solutions I've given you. It's better for all concerned. And, if anything else happens and you survive? Don't concern yourself. Many layers of security surround me. Don't waste your time."

The two men stared at each other a moment. Jim knew he'd sent the message he wanted. The man used the word don't twice, maybe without realizing it. Sometimes people's own words betray them.

"When you get your report on me, pay particular attention to what it says. And be very careful. Your security in this room is useless. Ask your bodyguard how he feels. You could have been dead many times over."

Ivanov glanced at his bodyguards and then gave Jim a curt nod.

As the group left, Alina paused at the door. He'd never seen her look so cold. She spoke in a soft voice. "Your advantage is the forest. Stay home." After a parting look, she then disappeared into the lobby.

"That woman gives me the willies."

He glanced at Rita, glad to be looking at someone he considered normal. Contrasting the two, he wondered how he could have given Alina a second glance.

Rita's voice was puzzled. "What did she mean...stay home?"

THIRTEEN

BACK AT RITA'S VEHICLE, they sat watching the long, black limo pull away from the curb. It looked as if the boss had gathered all his players and left. Maybe. Jim didn't think he'd get very far trusting Anton Ivanov.

"So, the comment? Stay home?"

He thought a moment, gazing after the retreating limo. "She knows me, at least this much. I figure she thinks there will still be problems. The warning is to not take the fight to them on their own turf. Make them come to me. It makes a little sense if anything about this whole thing does."

She nodded. "If you say so. I'm not sure about any of this. In the meantime, take me to lunch?"

"Let's try Cheddar's. It's not noon yet, so it shouldn't be too busy."

They made the trip down Glenstone Avenue in silence, with only a few outbursts from Rita about idiot drivers. The parking lot wasn't too full, but when they went inside, the blast of noise from the crowd and background music met them. It was a wall of sound. She grabbed his hand and led him back outside.

They wound up at the Outback Steakhouse and found a quiet booth in a corner. A bustling waitress appeared immediately. He peered at her name tag. "Good morning, Darian. Just water for the lady and I'll have iced tea…unsweetened."

Rita stopped her. "I'll have a cola, whatever you have. Thank you."

"Sorry. I thought you'd be a water drinker."

"It's not a water kind of day. You don't know me, Jim. You should remember that. Although we put up a united front to Ivanov, that's all it was. A front."

He glanced at her, holding up his hand. "Hey, whoa up, girl. It's just lunch. Two people who gotta eat. I got it."

Darian was back momentarily with their drinks.

Rita buried her head in the menu for a moment and then laid it aside. They both ordered a rib-eye with loaded baked potato and salad.

"Great choice, folks. It'll be just a few minutes."

Watching the girl hurry to another table, Rita sighed and then looked at him until he met her gaze. "I met a man yesterday."

Jim paused with his sweetener hovering over his glass of iced tea and stared at her a long few beats. "Wow. My luck with women is downright dismal. I thought maybe…you and me?"

She didn't respond, just stared at him, and he faltered ahead. "Okay. Well, that didn't go well. Lighten up, will you?"

He watched her a moment. Her expressions were like reading a book, going from surprise to embarrassment and then on to acceptance.

"You dummy." She smiled at him. "I have to learn this about you. You're either all in, or all out, aren't you? I'm flattered, I guess. Look, you need to get your head out of your ass. So, your girl wasn't what you expected and didn't act the way you thought she should. It's clear her idea of commitment isn't the same as yours. Now you know. It didn't work out. Get over it."

She was poking the table with her index finger with every point she made. "Most women will seldom act the way their men think they will. And vice versa. You should learn to talk and then accept the answers. The answers may not be what you're looking for, but you should accept it. That's the only way to know what's going on. Once you do that, you can decide if you want to get serious. The strong silent type of macho BS will only get you in trouble."

Her strong opinion surprised him a little until he remembered she and her late husband had been in the military. He gave her a nod. "Talking is fine, I get that. But I'm more of the watch what people do, not what they say kind of guy."

He sat back and crossed his arms. "So, cheating is acceptable in your little book of life? What happened between Alina and me was just a lack of communication?"

She laughed and then leaned forward on her arms, folding her hands together. "No, cheating is never okay. I'm just saying a little conversation might have uncovered that little proclivity of hers a lot sooner and saved One-Ball some pain, not to mention the fact he sent a hitman after you."

He thought about that. Did he go to violence too soon? He thought of an old adage—girls talk, men act.

"No. I'm thinking she would have lied, regardless. No amount of talking would change that. It's just her nature. I don't think people can change who they are."

"Look, Jim." She smiled wider as his arms came to rest on the table, putting their heads closer together. "I don't know how long you were out in the boonies before you moved to the lake, but it must have been a long time. You can't be falling in love with every woman that parks her butt in front of you."

She paused as Darian brought each of them a house salad. Rita poured a liberal amount of ranch dressing over hers and offered him the Thousand Island without asking. He took it, ignoring her smirk. Was he that predictable?

"Number one." She pointed her fork at him. "You and I haven't made any sort of commitment. Since Johnny died, I haven't been on a date or alone with a man. Ever. We've only been talking to each other a few days."

"We've known each other for a couple of years." His tone sounded defensive and he didn't mean it to be that way. He could admit, to himself anyway, that he was moving fast. But in his mind, if you see something that's worth the risk—it's a risk you need to take.

"No, we've known *of* each other and you knew Johnny. You've seen me around enough to say howdy, that's about it. You had Alina, and for the last year I was getting over my own tragedy."

"Well, like you pointed out earlier. She wasn't around all that much." He was in uncharted territory and didn't quite know how to proceed. All he knew was whatever he'd felt for Alina didn't come close to what he was beginning to feel for this woman. Maybe she was right.

"Rita, please look at me." He waited until she met his

gaze. "Have you ever met someone that took your breath away every time you see them? Someone that makes you lose all train of thought or reason and you can't explain it?"

"Yeah." Her eyes lost focus a moment. "There was this stripper in New Orleans..."

His frustration started to boil to the surface and he pushed it down. "I'm serious. When you were married to Johnny, I buried that feeling, but every time we met, I felt it."

She looked at him and then examined her hands. "Maybe this feeling you have will go away like a virus or a bad rash." When he didn't reply, she sighed and pointed to his salad. "Eat."

Watching him chase a tomato around in his salad bowl, she picked up her original thread of conversation. "This guy I mentioned wouldn't be a romantic interest, although he's handsome enough."

"So?" He hoped his faked indifference wasn't too obvious. She pointed her fork at him and he wondered if he'd have ranch dressing on his nose.

"He's the Viktor I asked about in the meeting. He was asking questions about a friend of his that he was supposed to meet. The friend is missing." A frown crossed her face for a moment as she looked at him. "Alleged friend."

He decided some misdirection wouldn't hurt. "Handsome, huh?"

She nodded and then grinned at him. "Like one of those Russian diplomats you see in the old movies that wear a monocle and carry a saber."

"Ah. That guy. Set your heart to fluttering, did he?"

"Yeah, he did. But not in a good way. More like a

snake watching a mongoose." She shook her head, turning serious. "He's dangerous and big trouble. He was asking a lot of questions."

She paused, watching him. "And I was serious about that stripper."

"Male or female?" He laughed as her face turned red.

Darian appeared with their meal. "Everything okay here?"

"Couldn't be better, young lady. Couldn't be better."

———

AN HOUR later they were walking in the Battlefield Mall, using their trip to the big city to advantage and doing some shopping. She stopped in front of Victoria's Secret.

"See anything you like?" Rita peered in the front windows at the displays. "Sometimes a man's opinion is helpful."

Watching her, he gave an honest answer. "I do."

She looked at him in the reflection of the window. "Stop it. This isn't helping anything." The beginnings of a smile on her face took the sting from the comment.

"Well, I know men and women don't think alike. You made that very clear. Here's a man's opinion. Everything in there is to enhance the look of a woman's body. It's to put a pretty wrapping on you with a little bow so you can show off your...attributes."

People passed around them like water around rocks in a stream, but neither of them noticed.

"Rita, I just can't imagine you'd need any of that. The most beautiful thing you could ever wear is...nothing."

Her hand came up between her breasts as she looked

at him. He was conscious of her chest rising and falling as their gaze locked in a primal duel.

When she turned to him, the movement trapped his hand between her arm and her breast. He kept eye contact as he withdrew his hand, extending the contact with her for a long moment.

She shook her head, but her smile looked soft and wondering. "Damn you."

FOURTEEN

THE RETURN TRIP to his cabin was quiet. Rita drove slower and seemed to concentrate on the road. She would smirk at him occasionally and he supposed she was pulling his chain by being careful.

Her radio crackled on occasion, but it was all traffic stops and drunk boaters. All in all, it seemed to be a quiet day in paradise. She broke the silence, speaking loud over the road noise. "So, what's the plan? Is there anything going on this week at Club Lane on the Lake?"

Watching the landscape passing by was mesmerizing, and it took a moment to realize she'd spoken. "I'm sorry...what?"

She tried again. "Boy, were you lost in space. I asked what your plans are now that things are settled?"

Jim was trying to compose a good answer when he saw them pulling into his place. The smile he gave her was forced and he couldn't shake the feeling of impending doom. He'd read that was a symptom of an imminent heart attack. Maybe that would solve all his problems. She reached over and put her index finger on the button, unlocking the glove box so he could retrieve his Glock.

After a serious glance from Rita as she settled back into her seat, he spoke softly. "Look. I'm sorry about pushing you so hard. Personally, I mean. I was out of line. Except for the meeting with Ivanov, I had a great time today and I appreciate the company. And like you said, I'm all in with what I want. Sometimes, well...a lot of times, that gets me in trouble."

"You said it's settled?" He looked at the surrounding forest and somehow it didn't look as friendly as before. "I don't trust those people. They were lying. This isn't over. Not by a long shot. Take care, Rita."

She put her hand out to stop him. "Jim, wait. I've always been good at reading people. You just turned into someone different and I don't know how to read you. Is something wrong? I thought we were getting on pretty well. Talk to me."

"We're getting on fine. This isn't about us." He shook his head and waved his hand at the forest. "Too many memories, I guess. The scaries come out sometimes and I can't put them away. I get moody. Plus, I've a gut feeling things are going to get bad. You should follow your own instincts and stay away from me."

Even in the sunshine, the lake looked flat and gray to him. The shadows of the forest seemed dark. He looked around again, sighing and shaking his head.

"It's not safe."

Rita reached out to him. "I'll take that chance, Jim. If you don't think it's safe, then we need to find out why." When he didn't answer, she tried again. "Hey, there's a dance Saturday night. Maybe that will pull you out of your gloom-and-doom attitude. Are you going to be in town?"

He grinned at her. "You asking me out on a date?"

She shook her head. "No, but if you're there, maybe we'll meet up? I wouldn't mind a few dances. We'll see how it goes."

His smile faded and Rita felt bad. What was going on? It seemed like both were chasing each other while trying to avoid capture.

"Listen, Jim. I'm sorry I keep sending you mixed signals. For some reason, I'm like a teenager with hormones flying in every direction. I like you, but my thoughts are like the old whack-a-mole game. I'm my own worst enemy right now. I swear if I started having hot flashes, I'd think I was going through the change. Give this some time, okay? Besides, I'm distracted by all the Russians in your playpen."

"As you wish." He climbed out of the vehicle, put the pistol in his back pocket, and walked to his front door without a glance back at her. When he opened the front door, his hand swept back and pulled his pistol out.

Startled by his actions momentarily, she noted he didn't hold his gun in the classic two-hand grip to enter the house. He held his gun by his side as his other hand pushed the door open and she wondered at the skills this man must have that she knew nothing about. She was out of the vehicle in seconds to come up behind him. Through the open door, she could see his place was a mess.

He whispered, "Stay here."

She placed her back against the log wall and watched the landscape around them for movement, but her mind was inside with Jim. He cleared the place in about five minutes and called for her to come in. Standing in the living room, he gazed at the mess around him.

"This looks like somebody has a serious mad going." She stated the obvious as she looked around. Someone emptied all the drawers on the floor and flipped over the chairs and couch. "Maybe Alina came back with some friends?"

"More likely those players in the field Tony One-Ball talked about." He pointed to his gun safe mounted to the wall. The door looked like someone tried to pry it open. Jam marks and scratches marred its shiny surface. "Alina wouldn't do that, she'd know better. This was someone else. So far, I don't see anything missing and that worries me."

"I could get someone out here. Might be prints on the safe?"

He shook his head and walked away.

She was still looking around when she saw him open the sliding door to the deck. He started to go through and froze—heard his agonized voice.

"Ah...Boney?" Then his shoulders slumped as he went out on the deck. She found him on his knees. The dog was dead, covered in blood.

His hand caressed the dog's head. Nothing else needed saying. His voice was soft and she could hear the pain. She knew he loved that dog.

"He was getting old and slow, didn't like to run much anymore. I always figured that red boar would get him, or one like him. That's why I always put his cut-vest on him. I never figured on anything like this."

She did a quick look around and didn't see anything. Who could do such a thing? They'd stabbed the dog several times, like someone losing control. She sighed and put her hand on his shoulder. She felt him tense up, felt him shake a moment fighting back emotion that she knew would be better let out.

"I'm so sorry, Jim."

Her touch snapped him out of his stupor. He stood and reached inside the door, retrieving an old poncho to cover Boney with. She reached for him again and he shook his head, pulling away from her. He began looking at the floor of the deck. Close to the steps leading to the side of the house was a bloody bootprint.

Her voice was soft. "Already saw it. Won't tell us much."

He nodded. All it told him was the killer wore boots, not running shoes or deck shoes. It wasn't much, but he'd be looking at a lot of feet from now on.

Stepping inside the door, he opened the gun safe and took out the shotgun, stuffing his pocket with extra loads.

She'd followed him inside. "Jim, what are you... What the hell kind of loads are those?"

He paused loading the shotgun, showing her one. "It's the PDX1 Defender—has a rifled slug surrounded by double-ought buckshot. They're called zombie loads and designed to ruin someone's day."

Shaking her head, she examined the shotgun shell. "Like a regular load wouldn't? Jim, you've got to get yourself under control. I don't like what I'm seeing here."

"Let's just say this will stop someone with extreme prejudice." He slung the gun over his shoulder and started out the door. "And I am under control. I'll be back."

He looked back and Rita was staring at him. "Don't worry, I'm just going to look around."

It seemed odd to walk through the trees and not hear

Boney's paws padding along beside him. He shook off the melancholy and bent to the task. The rain from the day before helped and in his first semi-circle around the house, he picked up a trail right away. It didn't go far.

Whoever paid him a visit parked down the road, just out of sight. When approaching the house, they took little effort to avoid the occasional muddy spot. He kneeled by one spot that showed three footprints. It was enough.

When he returned, she was in his bedroom putting clothes back into his chest of drawers. He'd called out so she wouldn't be spooked. She spoke when he came in the door.

"I'm just guessing where things go. Everything still looks clean...I mean...they didn't soil anything. It looks like they were just making a mess."

He noticed she was wearing gloves. "So, where did you put my Victoria's Secret stuff?"

She looked as if she couldn't decide if he was serious, or maybe crazy. "I didn't see..."

Leaning against the doorjamb, he shrugged. "Damn. I bet they stole it. What am I supposed to wear now? I love the feel of silk."

"Idiot. I wouldn't doubt it. How can you joke at a time like this?"

She finished what she was doing and slid the drawers closed. By that time, he was sitting on the bed watching her, so she settled in beside him. "I didn't hear the Zombie Apocalypse start. Find anything?"

He nodded. "Yeah. Some. It was one guy who isn't very big. His stride is about two feet and his weight didn't make him sink much into the soft ground. I'd say about a hundred-sixty pounds. He has a nice new pair of cowboy boots with a pointed toe and zero tread on the front—dress boots. That smooth sole just might keep bloodstains a while. It looks like he parked up the road and then walked in for the main show."

"Sure it wasn't a woman?"

"Pretty sure." He paused a moment staring out the window at the lake. "I don't know many women, but I can't think of any of them who would kill a dog like that. This guy is a special kind of mean."

"That's some good intel for a stroll through the woods. Did he leave his name in the mud too?"

"In a way, he did." At her questioning look, he shrugged. "He didn't scribble his name in the mud, but I'm betting he drives a big black SUV with tinted windows. Maybe dealer plates? The owner will speak with an accent."

They buried Boney at a flat place down by the shore. The soil wasn't deep, so they piled rocks on top of the grave to keep the coyotes away.

Rita stood by him a moment and then stepped to the water to wash dirt from her hands. "Should we say something?"

He looked at her and shook his head. "I wouldn't know what to say. He was a good dog."

"Then that's enough."

She stayed with him until they got his place put back to normal. He tossed a couple of broken chairs on the fire pit. Neither spoke. They just weren't in the mood. He was outside cleaning the deck with a high-pressure water nozzle when she came to him.

"I'd better get going. Just in case you're wrong, I need to do some research on who's around here that's done something like this. There might be a record."

When he looked at her and saw she was serious, his voice turned grim. "It's a waste of time, and it won't be someone who used to pull wings off dragonflies and drown cats. I know who did it. Besides, I thought you were quitting the job?"

"I don't know." Shaking her head, she looked at him. "All things considered, I'm not sure I can. There's too much going on right now." She reached out and touched his arm. "Maybe you'd better come and stay with me? You said yourself that it's not safe here."

He didn't mean to startle her, but his look made her step back a pace.

"You go on. And thanks. I appreciate your help more than you know. But I'll be staying here. Maybe I'll do some hunting in the morning."

FIFTEEN

RITA WHEELED her Jeep into the bi-directional street surrounding the White Rock courthouse and Limestone County Seat, barely missing a kid on a skateboard being pulled by another on a bicycle. She honked her horn at them and received a middle-finger salute as they careened down the street.

She thought about capturing the boys for their disrespect and perp-walking them to jail. But the image of her in hot pursuit, lights flashing and siren blaring chasing two kids using a bicycle and skateboard as their getaway vehicles kept her from doing it. It did bring a smile to her face.

Bounding up the marble steps of the courthouse, she turned toward the conference room reserved for the county commissioners. Melissa, the secretary and keeper of the inner sanctum, yelled at her. "You can't go in there. They're in a meeting."

Rita responded with a wave. "Good."

When she went through the doors, she hoped the surprise and shock didn't show on her face. Jimmy

John Boyd was the sole commissioner sitting at the table and was as country hick as his name implied. He was also the elected head of the county commissioners. If this were an official meeting, there should be at least two more to make a quorum. Next to him sat Ted Sanders, her chief deputy. Bob Detwiler, with his usual superior smirk, sat across from them, resplendent in his full-dress highway patrol uniform. She figured he bought the medals and wondered if there was a stolen valor law for law enforcement like there was for armed services.

At the head of the table, sitting like he owned the place, was Viktor Kumarin.

What the hell? Jim's prediction of things getting worse settled like a malignant tumor in her mind. "Is this an official meeting of law enforcement or are y'all just hanging out?"

She pinned her chief deputy with her gaze. "Ted? Aren't you supposed to be serving warrants today? We finally get enough evidence to charge that child molester Fontaine, and your ass is parked in the courthouse? You need to hit the road."

The men stared at her. When there was no response, she put her hands on her hips. "All right, what's going on?"

"We thought you were on vacation for two weeks." Jimmy John indicated a chair. "Since you're here, you'd better sit down, Rita."

Rita? Not Sheriff?

"I'll just stand right here if you don't mind. I have a feeling this won't take long. Is this official business?" Her mind raced as her eyes studied each actor in this little play.

He cleared his throat, looking at the other men and then meeting her gaze. "Yes, it is."

"It can't be. You need the other two commissioners present. That's the law, Jimmy John." Not sure what was going on, she went on the offensive. "If you think this is official, then where are the others? Why wasn't I informed of the meeting? You have to post the meeting time. There are rules you have to abide by."

She paused a moment and then pointed at the Russian. "And what in the hell is Viktor with a K doing here?"

"Dammit, Rita. Just shut the hell up." Jimmy John dragged his hand over his face as if trying to remove a mask. "Mr. Kumarin has filed a complaint about a missing person and your failure to act."

"Is that a fact?" She ignored Kumarin. "And just where would that report be?"

No one at the table would meet her gaze. "Show me the paper. No? Don't have one? How strange is that? Look, this man inquired about a supposed friend of his that he couldn't locate. To my knowledge, he has never filed a missing person's report, or any kind of report—or shared where he was from—or specifically anything a two-year-old with a plastic badge and cap-gun would think to provide, present company included."

Bob Detwiler spoke up to fill the silence. "He also states that a man has been killed and you're covering it up."

"Who gives a shit what HE states?" She felt cold and repressed a shiver. "Those are very serious charges. So, again. There haven't been any reports of unexplained deaths, bodies, or people missing. No evidence of that at all. Show those to me and I'll act on them. Maybe Kumarin should explain how he knows all this. If someone died, and only Mr. Kumarin knows about it, then I would think, *Bob*, you'd be questioning *him*."

When she emphasized his name, the patrol officer's gaze dropped to the table. When she looked around, they all looked uncomfortable. All except the Russian. He was smiling.

Jimmy John cleared his throat again. "Look, Rita. We know you've decided to turn in your resignation. I'd like to have that now. I think it's best for all concerned."

How the hell did they know that? Agnes?

"Just like that? Right out of the blue, with no reason?" She settled her gaze on Kumarin. "Don't you boys feel just a little bit manipulated?"

A sudden epiphany hit her in the gut, and her shoulders slumped for a moment. Her voice was soft as she looked at them. "Has money changed hands here? You've been bought?"

The table erupted with everyone shouting at her with denials—all except Kumarin. He still smiled.

Jimmy John got the other two men to shut up. "That's it. Rita, effective immediately, you're fired. And don't start arguing. We appointed you to take over your late husband's term. We can un-appoint you. It's legal."

"Legal? Hardly. Not until you have a legal meeting and file with the court it isn't. Until then, I'm still the sheriff. It doesn't look to me as if legality is a high priority here. If it were, you'd have M'liss in here officially taking notes. So all this is under the table, and I doubt you'd want any *legal* investigative body in here looking at things. Maybe a little lawsuit of my own would shed some light on this."

She looked at all their faces. "So, in your little fantasy world, who takes over? Have you appointed Kumarin yet? I can't see the locals around here learning Russian, but with enough money spread around, I guess it could happen."

Jimmy John slapped his hand on the table. "All right. We'll get your court order, Rita. When we do, you're gone. It's not any of your concern, but the commission will take over your administrative duties, and State will help fill in with patrol." He paused a moment. "Ted will be appointed interim sheriff until we can hold the election."

She laughed outright. "Ted, huh?" When she looked at him, he wouldn't meet her gaze. "Couldn't get in my pants, so you get my job instead? You're pathetic. Y'all have a good day, hear? And boys? Enjoy your newfound wealth."

The commissioner held out his hand. "I'll have your badge. Your gun too."

"Nope. The badge stays until the court order. This is my private weapon and I have a permit for it. You'll find I hold a civilian concealed carry permit, and open carry is legal in this state. So, kiss my ass, Jimmy John.

"You know? I'm kinda curious." She looked around at them one last time. "What's the going price? How much did it take?"

She thought of dropping a pin on the table to see if she could hear it. If she had a grenade, that might have been a better choice. Her gaze finally settled on Kumarin. "This isn't Russia—you don't get to take my weapon. I might need it to shoot something. Maybe a skunk or a snake. They smell about the same sometimes. Seems I'm getting a distinct odor right now."

She stalked from the room, slamming the door so

hard Melissa spilled her coffee. "Did you hear all that, M'liss?"

"Yeah, I did." The girl stood and was busy wiping coffee off her dress. "I'd count yourself lucky, even if it is a forced vacation. There's weird stuff going on around here, and I'm thinking of taking some time off myself."

She stopped wiping long enough to look at Rita. "Talk to Agnes."

———

A FEW MINUTES LATER, Rita was sitting on a concrete bench in front of the war memorial, just off to the side of the courthouse. The long list of those having served always seemed to calm her. It was said once that a caretaker found an old man sitting among the grave-stones in a national cemetery. When asked why he was sitting out there all alone, the man gestured at all the white marble, row by row, and said he wasn't alone.

She sighed, taking deep, calming breaths and thinking of the Vietnam veterans. "Well, boys and girls. The politicians did it again. They wouldn't let you win. It's not looking good for me, either."

The afternoon sun was warm on her shoulders. A skateboard clattered down the sidewalk a half block away. She thought of giving chase just for the fun of it.

"Rita."

Startled, she looked around and saw Kumarin walking up to her. She regarded him a moment, hand on the butt of her pistol, and then turned away. "What the hell do you want?"

"Just so you know, all I did was inquire about a

missing person. Your deputy—or ex-deputy, I guess—took it from there. I have no ill will toward you."

Yeah, right. "Okay. That's good to know."

She turned to him and met his cold gaze. "You're lying, and we both know it, but thanks for the effort. Now, if you don't mind, I'm communing with the spirits here."

He looked at the memorial and gave her an odd glance. "Which war?"

"All of them."

"Yes. Well. Too bad your government leaders decided they could make more money by losing than winning." Almost coming to attention, he nodded. "You wish to be alone. After the spanking you got inside, I can understand that. As you wish. We should always honor our dead."

"Do you? Honor your dead?"

The man stood a moment, seeming to consider the question and then nodded. "If they deserve it."

"Wait." She pointed across the street. "Who are those men?"

Kumarin smiled at her. "Those are friends of the missing person. No one seems to care about him, but we do. We shall conduct a search."

"What's your game here? What do you want from this town?" When he didn't answer, she continued. "Maybe if you told someone the missing person's information, you'd have better luck, don't you think?"

"Why would you care? As you put it, you're out of the game, so you should not worry yourself. Still, there's no reason we can't be friends." He smiled at her and walked away.

"Wait a minute. Do you know Anton Ivanov? I understand he told you to go home."

He didn't acknowledge her question. Her instincts told her he was dirty. She knew it, but didn't have anything to hang her hat on. She should talk to Agnes. This was getting complicated in a damned big hurry. And he was right. She was out of the game. Sort of.

Her gaze followed Kumarin as he walked, and it registered where he was walking. Three black SUVs parked together with heavily tinted windows. The angle of the sun allowed her to see shadows inside the vehicles. They all looked full of people. At the minimum twelve, maybe more. Her thoughts turned to a cabin by the lake and a man with a dead dog.

This was going to get ugly. Now she had no authority to help. At least, not officially. Technically, she was still the sheriff. The badge was for show. The question was... who would jump when she barked.

Another question piled onto the ever-growing stack. How much influence could a group of men with no scruples and lots of money have on a poor, impoverished community? She'd already seen some of it. And control is what the Russian mob specialized in.

Dammit.

SIXTEEN

MORNING DAWNED COOL AND DAMP. The weather channel's forecast predicted a cold spring. A week before they'd predicted a warmer-than-normal spring. Jim figured they had at least a fifty percent chance of being right.

It was dark inside his house, and he stood well away from his back window, searching the forest across the inlet with a pair of binoculars. Someone tried to kill him and knifed his dog to death. So, who? Anton Ivanov said he and his men were out of the game. Did he believe him? Somehow, he did. If that was true, then who was pulling the strings? It was possible something outside of Ivanov's control was going on.

Tony? He'd be surprised if Tony wasn't on a very short leash, but it could be.

Alina? He couldn't see it. A comment made at the meeting came back to him. An asset in the field. In this day and age, he couldn't fathom anyone being out of communication unless they wanted to be. So, a rogue?

This situation seemed to be more than one of Ivanov's

soldiers not getting the word in time. They'd be on a short leash too. And any criminal enterprise demanded loyalty. So, someone was still active. The big question was how they would play it without attracting too much attention to themselves. What happened to Boney, and the trashing of his house, was intended as intimidation. Clearly, that didn't work. But assuming the laws of unintended consequences, they did have his undivided attention from now on.

He hadn't seen Rita since she left. She'd mentioned a man came to see her—a Viktor Kumarin. He couldn't tell if she was afraid of him—or fascinated by him. His mind was on that man as he laced his boots. Another Russian. A new player? He remembered the mob boss talking to Tony Kumarin, and he'd been agitated about his using someone in the field. Was he uncontrollable? The question was why? He agreed with Rita on one point. There were too damned many Russians showing up.

On impulse, he decided to go to breakfast in White Rock and nose around a little. Maybe he'd visit Agnes. She'd know something. Twenty minutes later, he skidded to a stop in the parking lot of the sheriff's office.

Agnes Benson, rumored to rule her children and grandchildren with a loving iron fist, sat in front of her array of 911 computer screens. But her headset was on the counter in front of her because she had her nose buried in a magazine.

A man sat at the duty desk behind her and in the center of the room. Barney Jones looked like the legendary Barney Fife from the old *Andy Griffith* series. Jim wondered how many bullets were in the big Smith & Wesson revolver at his hip.

"Hey, Barnes," he greeted the man with more familiarity than he felt.

The reply was just as friendly. "Hey Jim, how's it going? Still pulling in crappie by the boatload?"

He grinned at the man. "Yep. I just set the bucket up front, and they jump right in. I do have to slow down some on windy days. It throws them off somehow."

A muffled, sexy voice came from behind the magazine. "Liar."

Jim sidled over and pulled up a chair next to her. "Hey, Agnes. What's new?"

She lowered the magazine and looked at him. Then she spoke over her shoulder. "We need some coffee, Barney. How's about making a run?"

The deputy pointed toward a coffee pot percolating on a back table. "But we got—"

"Now, Barney."

The man wasn't stupid. He left, rolling his eyes at Jim.

Jim tried again. "I guess Rita kept you up to date?"

She picked up the magazine again, looking disinterested. "About what?"

"You know, there are some new people around. I'm wondering if you have any information on them. Knowing about this Viktor Kumarin would be my first choice."

The magazine dropped again as she scanned her screens. "Look, Jim. I like you. Rita likes you too. But she has enough trouble of her own right now and does not need help in stirring up more. In the meantime, why don't you cool it for a while? Now that she's ready to get back in the game, she needs to look around at what's available. I'm not real sure you're a good fit for her. She's a little confused right now."

He looked at her for a moment, hoping his rising anger didn't show. "Funny, I thought we were talking about Russians, not your advice to the lovelorn column in the who cares section of the paper. And to your point, she didn't look too confused the other day. But, hey. I get my signals crossed sometimes. Next time I decide to talk to her, I'll call you first. Sound good?"

Staring at her and shaking his head, he continued. "I'd like to get the conversation turned back to strangers lurking about. Is there anything you can help me with?"

A non-911 call interrupted them. Agnes talked a moment and assured the caller she'd send someone right over. Hanging up, she keyed the radio.

"Barney."

He came back within a few seconds.

"Go with traffic."

She looked over at Jim and grinned.

"Mabel called...something about an animal."

There was a few seconds pause, and then he acknowledged.

"Ten-three."

She looked at him. "It's been a pretty exciting day so far. Mabel is Barney's girlfriend, and he's been on night shift. I think the animal problem is her kitty. If you get my drift. Ah, well. Life in a small town."

"I take it you aren't going to talk to me about anything except stray cats, Rita's blooming love life, and me staying away from her?"

"You're not law enforcement, so you have no need to know what's going on in the county. I'm sorry about your dog and someone trashing your place, but you gotta understand that's not a huge priority around here." She must have realized how that sounded. "Mabel's kitty notwithstanding."

So, Rita hadn't told her about the alleged killing. Interesting. He wondered what Rita's angle was—what she had on her mind. If there was anyone around smart enough to figure things out, it would be her. "Fine, I can take a hint."

She just stared at him a moment and smiled. "You'll get your ducks in a row soon enough. Besides, even if I did know something—I don't spread rumors."

He shook his head. "Right. Okay, then. I guess I'll see you around." He sat a moment longer, trying to piece together all the bits of information she wasn't telling him. "Did Rita say if she's going to the dance tonight?"

"Jim, please don't..." She placed her headset on the table after scanning her screens. "Give the woman some room to maneuver, will ya? She's trying to figure some things out, and they're not all personal. You're clouding the issue."

He knew his expression was taking confused to a new level. "From what Rita told me, I thought you were on my side. Kinda pushing her toward me."

She wouldn't meet his gaze, watching screens. "I'm on her side. Anything else regarding the county is none of your damn business."

He stood, dragging the chair back to its proper spot. "I get it. You know, it's still sort of a free country, even though some of you seem to be flying a Russian flag. At least you won't have to worry about standing for the National Anthem anymore. Bye, Agnes."

"Go to hell, Lane. I don't know why I ever liked you." She stopped him before he got to the door and then pulled him outside. "Jim, listen to me. There are things going on here that I never thought I'd see. The word is, we should ignore certain things and certain people, and big money will show up for us."

After looking around the parking lot, she squinted against the sunlight, staring into his face. "Don't take anything at face value. And if it comes down to it, you take care of that girl. She ain't as tough as she makes out."

After she went back inside, he stood a moment. Was she bipolar? She acted like there were listening devices around. He went from confused, through thoughtful, to downright concerned. What the hell was going on?

––––––

JIM'S next stop was the Café for breakfast. When he stepped inside, he was looking around the crowded eatery for an empty table when he saw Rita sitting with someone. Anger replaced the hunger gnawing at his stomach and his appetite left.

Right behind the flash of anger came bewilderment because there was no reason to be angry—she could sit with whomever she wanted. He thought about going to the doctor for an industrial-strength antacid—or tranquilizer. Maybe a pill to get him out of his junior high thought processes. Somehow, he had to get his head screwed on straight.

Moving toward them, something looked odd. Acquaintances sharing a table will sit across from each other to give a little room. Or if sitting side by side, at least move away from each other—not invading personal space and giving a little elbow room for the actual mechanics of eating.

She was sitting shoulder to shoulder with this guy. His temper started to boil again. This just under the surface anger concerning Rita was starting to worry him. He strolled over and sat down in front of them.

She looked up and flinched back in her chair. "Jim."

He nodded and waved away the waitress coming toward them, faking a good humor he didn't feel. "Hiya, Rita. Who's your buddy?"

He could see her trying to scoot her chair away from the man at her side, but the wood floor wasn't cooperating. Neither was the man. He'd shifted his position, and Jim figured he'd hooked his foot around her chair leg. Jim stared at her, but she wouldn't meet his eyes. Seemed to be a lot of that going around lately.

The man's hand came across the table as he stated the obvious. "I'm Viktor."

He stared at the man's hand a moment and then slowly considered the man's expressionless eyes. The term dead fish came to mind. He didn't know the game being played, but this was the real deal. He wondered if Rita knew this man was a killer.

"I thought you wore a monocle."

Her response was immediate. "Jim, you're being rude." She'd regained her composure and he could see a slight flush climbing out of her shirt collar. "You could at least be polite."

He was still in a staring match with Kumarin. The man was starting to smile.

"I don't think so. Polite is not on my list of things to do today."

That wiped the smile away. Kumarin pulled his hand back. "Why, Mr. Lane? I don't understand. We're not enemies. I think you know who I am and that I used to work for a certain benefactor in St. Louis. That is all in the past. Things will work out for all of us. There's no point in carrying on any hostility."

Jim nodded. "Oh, I'm sure you understand well enough. It's not who you are that concerns me, it's what you are. People like you never change, even if you change employers, get different clothes—hang out with different people. It doesn't change a thing. So, I don't have to shake your hand and I don't have to like you. It's that simple. Besides, your little game is still going on and we both know it. All in the past? Like, from a few days ago? Or today? I promised your boss I'd be fair about this, so here's your last chance. I'm serving notice right now. A one-time opportunity just for you. Leave. Now. The climate is not good for you here."

Rita gasped and Kumarin stood, skidding his chair backward.

"You threaten me?"

The surrounding conversation stopped. Jim wondered how many cell phones were recording. "Yep. Right here in front of the sheriff and all these good people. I'm still gathering information, but I've got almost everything I need. Things are becoming clear. I need to find one other player to make this little soap opera complete, and I'm thinking you know where to find him. Someone about five-nine or ten, wears new cowboy boots, and likes a knife? Have you seen that guy around? Maybe paid him some big money?" Jim shook his head at the man. "You've made a mistake, Kumarin. It may prove fatal."

The man appeared calm and his flat gaze settled on Jim. "With the proper resources, mistakes can always be rectified. We shall see."

"It'll be the last thing you ever see."

Kumarin scoffed. "You sound like the hero from one of your cowboy movies. You have no idea what you're getting into."

Jim shook his head, watching the man closely. "This ain't St. Louis, it's Limestone County. And one other thing. If you'd ever, and I mean *ever,* watched a western movie, you'd know better than to kill a man's dog." He paused to let that sink in. "When you talk to Anton Ivanov, and I'm sure you will, tell him to get his affairs in order—the deal is off. I keep my promises."

"Such bravado for your audience." Kumarin gave Rita a mocking half-salute. "I have no idea what you're talking about. Have a good day, Rita. I'll see you soon."

He watched Kumarin leave, never letting his hand move from the butt of his pistol. Following him to the door, he saw the Russian step into the passenger side of a black SUV, and they sped off. That was curious. Did he need a chauffeur to come to breakfast? Or was this simply one more thing to check off his list of things to do on this particular day? Was Rita on his check-off list?

He'd followed the Russian out the door to make sure he left and was getting into his truck when Rita caught up with him. Her face looked drained of color and he couldn't tell if it was anger or guilt—maybe she was sick. A toss-up, but it didn't matter. That train was leaving. Why does learning lessons always hurt, and this one especially so?

"Wait, Jim. Let me talk to you. You don't understand. There are things going on here that you don't know about. I was trying to—"

Looking at her, he couldn't find it in himself to be mad at her for very long. That was a different worry all its own. He felt sad as he interrupted. "Isn't it strange?

Women are always telling me that I just don't understand. Agnes told me that earlier this morning. You're telling me that now. I'm sure Alina would have told me that if she'd had the chance. But sooner or later, I figure it out. I'm not stupid, Rita. Dense? Yeah, sometimes. And I'll admit to being old-fashioned—sometimes to a fault. But I'm not stupid."

She tried again. "Jim, please just listen. Things are getting out of control."

"Well, I don't know what things you're talking about, but be careful they don't turn around and bite you." He'd always wanted to say it. "Sorry. Whatever you are into is not my circus—not my monkeys. Not anymore."

As he backed the truck out of the parking lot and hit the road, he looked in his rearview mirror. She was still standing there. He felt bad about lying to her, because deep down, he knew the circus was in town and the monkeys were running circles around the big top. It just may be monkey season.

SEVENTEEN

WHEN JIM RETURNED HOME, and after making sure there were no surprises waiting for him, his stomach let him know he'd missed breakfast. He threw together some cold cuts, bread, and grape jelly, and sat at his table to eat.

His mood was somber as he thought about Rita and her swashbuckler friend. He couldn't imagine the attraction there, but then he would never pretend to know the female mind. When things get too complicated, all a man can do is believe his eyes. He needed to figure out what his senses were telling him. The adage came to him. Don't dwell on what people say, watch what they do. That mostly pointed toward politicians, but it worked for everyone. Those were words to live by.

Finished with his meal, he washed down the instant bellyache with a beer. It burned all the way down.

He looked at his bookcase filled with the writings of Louis L'Amour. There were other authors, but this one writer shaped much of his thinking. If anyone cared, he'd be unapologetic for that. But he was sure no one did. He picked up a dog-eared copy of *Shalako*, and then put it back and selected *Last Stand at Papago Wells*. It suited his mood. Laden with a good book and his fishing tackle, he went down and fired up his bass boat.

Motoring out onto the lake to be out of range from anyone but a world-class shooter, he found a shallow spot, pitched his anchor and wet his hook. And it was just that. The hook had no bait on it. He relaxed with a good book. If he happened to take a nap? Well, there ya go.

Toward evening, refreshed from his rigorous afternoon of fishing, he motored up to his dock. Boney didn't come to meet him and that fresh sadness pissed him off. Unbidden thoughts of Rita slipped past his defenses and into his mind. That added to the fuel. She was a beautiful woman and he knew they'd both felt an attraction.

He indulged in one of his favorite pastimes—arguing with himself. So, their renewed friendship was only a few days old. How long does it take? She seemed to be pushing him away. Why? He figured she had her reasons —damned if he knew what they were.

Boredom finally got the best of him. Going to the dance was a toss-up between insanity and self-abuse but he decided to go anyway—maybe get in a dance or three. Two could play the game. Maybe he should expand his female horizons. There were always plenty of unattached ladies there.

When he arrived at the Old Barn, the parking lot was crowded. The rowdy noise of humanity having a good time spilled out the windows, and as he passed through the door, it was almost a physical blow. Someone had fixed up a giant old mule barn, complete with hardwood floors with a thin layer of sawdust, a bar, and tables to hold drinks. The tables were for couples. The looky-loos could lean on the bar or against the walls. The owners managed to hold festivities there about once a month.

The loud music got better sounding as beer kegs emptied. If you wanted something stronger than beer to drink, you brought your own—and shared once people saw it. It was hot inside and the exhaust fans mounted in the outside walls were churning hard.

Jim threw some money into the tip bowl for the band and stood against a wall, the usual spot for a man with no date. Dressed in boots and Dockers with a long-sleeved shirt and his denim vest, he enjoyed the sights and smiled at a few unattached girls glancing his way. It wasn't long before he saw Rita.

They'd made no promises and there was nothing between them, except maybe in his own mind. So why get churlish? He chided himself for coming in the first place and tried to rein in his feelings. His thoughts were going full throttle and he couldn't find the brakes. Dammit, this was stupid. A junior high crush looked a little strange on a forty-year-old. But she'd invited him...sort of.

Rita and Viktor were dancing a slow dance. Breakfast meeting and then a dance? There were inferences there he didn't want to think about, so it was definitely time to move on. It was obvious the Russian wasn't much of a dancer, but he didn't need to be. They weren't moving much, except against each other. And he knew she'd seen him, because she kept sending looks his way and slightly shaking her head. They weren't kind looks. Time to go.

As he watched, she stiffened and moved his hands away from her ass. The hands went back and stayed. Since she didn't shoot him, Jim figured that was consent.

He did a mental eye roll. This was stupid. It was time to get outta Dodge, as the old saying went.

The music ended, and for some reason he couldn't fathom, she was walking toward him with Viktor close behind. It was too late for a rescue if that's what she wanted. Jim moved his shoulders from his favorite wall and turned to leave. He'd been right all along. Self-abuse was humiliating.

Her voice was loud because the music started up again. "Hi, Jim. No date?"

He stopped to make a reply as he glanced at her, shrugged and started to walk away, and then stopped again.

Self-abuser. He might as well start cutting himself.

"No. No date. I kinda thought I had one lined up, but she couldn't wait and found a better deal. I think she traded down, but hey, that's just my opinion."

She pointed at him with her free hand. "We never had a..."

He held up his hands in surrender. "It's none of my business. Really. It's all right. I should have called." He glanced toward Viktor. "But with this? I'm sorry. I don't play games. I'm not good at it. So, y'all enjoy your evening and I'll mosey on out of here."

Rita reached out for him. "Would you like to dance? Please? We can talk."

He started to answer when he saw Kumarin nod to someone across the room. That made his internal alarm bells start ringing. As far as he knew, the Russian didn't know anyone here. That nod surprised him. He turned away from them, looking at the crowd. The music stopped and the emcee announced a break.

When the crowd shuffled from the floor, Jim saw him.

A slim man with black, slicked-back hair and pallid complexion was moving toward them—a man with an off-the-rack western look to him, including a shiny new pair of boots. And a hat too big for him. He was like an artist's rendition of a cowboy, if the artist had never seen one.

With studied nonchalance, he turned back toward Rita. But he was on full alert, wondering how to get a look at the bottom of the man's boot. One idea came to mind, but he didn't have an excuse to flat-back him. He needn't have worried. It came right away.

The man stopped in front of them, pushed Jim on the shoulder, and stepped back. "Were you staring at me?"

Jim couldn't help it and laughed. The wannabe bad man was trying to start a schoolyard fight. Well, he was in the mood for it. "Why? You something special? Look, dummy. I don't know who you are or where you're from, but you're going about this all wrong. If you want a piece of me, you don't have to put on a show and strut around like a little rooster. Just start the music. I'll try and dance the tune. And where in the *hell* did you get that hat?"

Rita tried to cut in. "Look, boys, there's no reason for this. Let's dial it down a little."

The man spoke loud over the noise. "He disrespected me. I can't allow that."

Up to now it must have looked to Rita and the spectators like a normal argument at a dance. Then the man stepped back and whipped up a long-bladed stiletto in his right hand. Homemade tattoos covered his muscular arms. With no warning, the knife swept upward in a move meant to bury the blade in Jim's heart, just under the sternum. It would have worked in a crowded room.

Jim heard a sharp cry from Rita as he slipped a half

step to the right and trapped the knife hand and forearm between his own arm and chest. They stood face to face as the man struggled to free his arm.

"You need a breath mint."

In a move so quick it seemed casual, Jim brought his left hand up inside the man's trapped arm and placed it on the man's shoulder making the arm and knife useless. "Uh, oh. Now what, shithead? Still wanna play?"

In his peripheral vision, he could see Viktor struggling with Rita. Her voice sounded desperate. "Dammit, let me go! Jim, stop this now! We can arrest..."

A shove from the side made him lose his hold on his assailant and cost him a slight cut across his ribs. That was his first mistake of the evening. Well, his second, if he counted showing up in the first place. The oldest fighting rule in the world was to watch your back. The enemy in front of you may not be the only one around.

Stiletto man stepped backward to give himself room while rubbing his arm. Assuming Rita didn't shove him, Jim turned and hit Viktor in the face with a straight punch. The man went down like a hammered steer.

Rita shrieked a warning and then stiletto man was coming for him.

Viktor bounced up and grabbed Rita again. It looked to Jim like she was trying to reach the holster she kept at the small of her back, but the Russian pulled her against him, keeping her arms pinned.

His mouth felt dry as an August creek bed knowing his own weapon was in his truck. Unarmed, and needing room to maneuver, he stepped farther out into the room.

Since Viktor interfered on the attacker's behalf, this had to be the other player—the one they couldn't call off.

So be it. Better now than in the dark somewhere. His voice carried to the man. "You can put your mind to rest."

The stiletto man circled and flourished his blade with a tight grin on his face. "What do you mean by that?"

Jim shrugged. "You won't be going back to prison, so you can take that worry off the table." The man held the weapon in his right hand, so Jim moved toward the right to limit the range of motion and effectiveness of the knife. As they circled, he shrugged from his leather vest and wrapped it around his left arm.

Not having made good on his surprise attack and now drawing a crowd, the man glanced around and looked unsure of himself. He stopped a moment.

"Why?" Then realizing his mistake, he blustered. "I ain't never been in prison."

"You're a lying little cockroach. You haven't seen daylight in years, and you don't look like someone who works in an office. Anyone can see it. How do you know Ivan?" He pointed his thumb over his shoulder at Viktor.

"His name ain't Ivan..." You could almost see the man mentally slap a hand over his mouth.

Jim was getting tired of this. Rita had stopped struggling so hard, watching the byplay. As they circled, he could see Viktor watching with a bloody smile with his arms encircling Rita. One of the musicians set down his guitar. The hollow clunking sound it made meant he'd missed its rack as he watched the show on the dance floor. The crowd surged into a large circle, and he once again felt country was the place he wanted to be.

The men wouldn't interfere in a fight between two men, and most of the women stood with their men. All were watching with interest. No fainting hearts here. He made eye contact with his adversary.

"You shouldn't worry about going back to prison because you won't be leaving here, at least not alive."

Laughing in a voice strained with tension, the man held up his knife. His eyes were several kinds of crazy. "See the stains on this, boy? It's doggy blood. You should have heard that dog howl. I'm going to add your blood to it. Then I'll go have a beer."

If the intention was to make Jim mad, it worked. He started toward the man when he heard someone off to the side say, "Let's even this thing up a little."

He glanced to the right, saw an object sailing his way, and snatched it out of the air. It was an old KABAR fighting knife with a heavy black blade sharp enough to shave with and a worn leather handle. He'd like to thank someone for it, but couldn't take his eyes away from the other man. Standing straight and relaxed, he unwrapped the vest from his arm and then tossed it away.

Stiletto man attacked. Jim sucked in his belly to avoid a wide sweep and parried a stab at his chest. He guessed his opponent used surprise for close work. Who knew how many men he'd shanked in prison that way? It showed in his whining frustration.

The man made more desperate attempts to kill him but looked to be out of ideas and moves. Every time they came together, Jim was sure to leave a cut on his arms. They circled in a macabre dance, but even in this, the man lost advantage. His boots were good for a boot-scootin'-boogie but clumsy for this dance. The sawdust floor was slick for a purpose. The man stepped back, breathing hard.

Jim stood, waiting on him. "What's your name? We'll need something for your headstone."

They lunged at each other, parrying for position. Both

men wound up holding each other's knife arm. Jim was taller and started using his height advantage to bring his blade toward the juncture of the man's throat and collarbone.

Stiletto man was strong and struggled hard, but dawning realization shone in his eyes. He gave a whining groan as he dropped his knife to use both hands against Jim's blade. The progress toward his throat was slow and inexorable.

The room wasn't quiet. He heard people breathing and gasping as they watched the primeval contest before them. The sound of Rita's voice rose above the others.

"Stop this now! Dammit, Viktor. Let me go!"

Distracted for a moment, he turned all his attention on the man before him. It was time to end it. Staring into the man's eyes, Jim leaned harder into him and the man's knees started to buckle. The point of the blade touched his throat and the man's panting breath was pulsing into his face.

He pleaded in a strained voice. "No...no..."

"This is for Boney."

He started to bury the knife when a blow to the head sent him to his hands and knees, his borrowed knife skittering across the floor. The roaring in his head pushed everything away.

The last thing he saw was Rita backing away from him, holding her pistol by the barrel. He tried to shake his head against the pain. Big mistake. His image of Rita was getting fuzzy as he thought he saw her shove Viktor away from her. As Jim fell to the floor, he had a thought.

Betrayal can only come from someone you trust.

———

A BLINDING white light pierced his brain and squinted his eyes shut. Something blocked the light, jostling him around. He opened his eyes again to see someone crouching over him. The safety belts on the stretcher strapped his arms down, and the man unsnapped the one across his chest for better access. He started to place a blood pressure cuff around the left arm. When the restraint came off, Jim reached over and grabbed the medic.

"How bad am I?"

The man bleated and jerked backward, winding up in the bench seat with one hand over his chest. Turning his head, he shouted, "Hey, Wayne. Don't take off yet." He turned back to Jim. "You scared the shit out of me."

The medic took a couple of deep breaths. "Okay, here's the deal. The sheriff whacked you on the back of the head during that little dust-up inside the dance hall. When you stayed unconscious for more than five minutes, they called us in."

Jim knew where this was heading. "I was just resting."

The medic looked askance at him. "Yeah. Sure you were." He continued, "Here's the deal. You have a shallow cut along your ribs that may need stitches, although a few butterfly strips might work if you take it easy."

"How'd you get here so quick?"

The man shrugged. "Something like this happens every time they have a dance. Pays to stay close."

He leaned forward and moved Jim's head to the side, checking something on the back. Pulling out a four-inch gauze pad, he showed it to him.

"See? No bleeding, so you're in good shape there.

We'll just run you to Springfield Mercy and get you checked out."

Jim sat up with a grimace. He paused a moment to get his balance and then unbuckled the straps across his legs. The back doors of the box-type ambulance were open, and he saw the front of the dance hall and a few people standing around. None seemed to be looking his way.

"Nope. I'm not going anywhere, but thanks for the help. I'm out of here."

The man had his hand on Jim's shoulder, trying to push him back down. "Wait, man. You might have a concussion. When we picked you up, you were out like a light. That hit scrambled your head good and turned your switch off. There could be swelling in your brain."

He shrugged the man's arm away and rattled the rail on the side of the gurney. "Take this down, please. Look, you don't have my permission to transport me. We both know what that means. You can't stop me, and I'm leaving."

Jim rolled his head side-to-side and instantly regretted it. "Besides, my head's been scrambled half my life and most folks don't think I have a brain."

"Well, considering what you're doing, they could be right." The medic sighed as he pulled a penlight from his pocket. "Look at me." He shined the light in both of Jim's eyes, making him squint again from the pain. "Your pupils are equal and reactive. You seem aware of your surroundings, although in some pain. I don't have a baseline to evaluate your sanity. You may have been insane before the blow, or it's a recent acquisition, but that's not one of the criteria to hold you."

He pulled down a clipboard, shuffled around, and

brought out a sheet of paper to put on top. "This is a refusal to transport. It's for my protection, not yours. If you die, I don't want someone coming back to fry my ass for letting you go. Sign it, and you're gone. I hope that's not a prediction."

Jim gave the man a half-smile, signed the document, and swung his feet over to stand up. After he banged his head on the ceiling, he stooped over and made his way out of the ambulance. Once out of the vehicle, he fought dizziness again and tried not to show it.

It took him a couple of minutes to find his truck, using the locator on the key fob. The medic had followed him and stood a few feet away.

"I'm okay, man. Thanks."

"Whatever you say." The medic shrugged and walked away.

HE STOPPED TWICE on the way home to pull off the road and throw up on the pavement. He met one car, seeing its headlights as foggy halos. The hospital was a better choice than where he was going, but there were greater risks with that decision than running around with a slight concussion.

He'd be helpless if tied down to a hospital bed in an environment he didn't control. They would ask questions he didn't want to answer. If the enemy was there, he didn't want to make things easier for them. It was obvious they were around.

There'd been two attempts on his life and he'd survived because he was on his own ground and very lucky. He wasn't going to give them the advantage by going to theirs. Alina had mentioned it as she left. Stay home. His advantage was out in the woods. Better to hide himself away and heal. Then he'd sort all this out.

When he got to his cabin, it took him a half hour to change into his camouflage clothes and hunting boots. A jacket and boonie hat completed his wardrobe. When he turned to leave, the room started spinning and he felt nauseous. He sat on the bed, trying to force the weakness away. A few moments later, he felt better and left the bedroom.

Old habits don't go away. In the past, he'd always needed to be ready to leave on a moment's notice. He kept a bag by the gun cabinet that was full of all the things he felt was necessary for survival. At least it was spring and the weather not too cold. He unlocked the gun safe and loaded up with more supplies.

He slung two pouches holding ammo for his pistol and shotgun over his shoulders. An extra .38 caliber revolver was clipped to his belt to supplement the Glock —insurance against a jamming autoloader. When he bent over to attach a boot knife, he almost fell. A white-hot pain knifed across behind his eyes, making him take a knee for a moment.

He stood in slow motion and resumed his task, leaving the M-4 and long guns. He wasn't out to fight a war. But in the close confines of the forest and brush, if they wanted one, he'd for damn sure answer the call, so he slung the shotgun over his shoulder.

Walking to the front door, he took one last look around and turned off the lights. Maybe he should just fort up here and see what happened? Maybe he should wait to see if Rita came to arrest him for punching her date. Maybe the Russians wouldn't try for him again.

Maybe, just maybe, the tooth fairy would come and make everything rainbows and butterflies—sing some campfire songs with him.

No. Rita made her choice. He needed to get away for a while and think—figure out his options. There would be blood in the future. Russian blood. Looking around, he hoped it wasn't the last time he'd see this place.

————

RITA LOOKED out the door of the dance hall and noticed the ambulance pulling away. Since they weren't using emergency lights, she assumed they thought Jim was okay and would take him to the hospital to be checked out. She'd see about him later when she got rid of her guilt trip. God, she was a fool. What had she done, using jealousy like a schoolgirl? She thought of the scarecrow singing "If I Only Had a Brain."

Then the situation got out of control. Where did that man come from? It had to be another attempt on Jim's life, but she couldn't let Jim kill the man. He'd go down for manslaughter or murder, and that wasn't fair. The law doesn't care who is right.

God, what a mess.

She turned and spoke to Barney, the deputy they'd assigned to the dance. "You know the commission is trying to get a court order to make me step down. Will you help me until they do?"

"You know I will."

She put a hand on his shoulder. "Get this piece of crap knife artist over to the jail. We'll book him later for attempted murder and disrupting a perfectly good dance...and there's no bail for that last one."

Several of the crowd laughed as they went over to the raised dais where the musicians were tuning their instruments.

Kumarin eased up to her and it seemed odd that he had the new wannabe acting sheriff in tow. When did he show up? "I will press charges against your boyfriend." He stood holding a handkerchief to his mouth. "I may need stitches."

She glanced from him to Deputy Sanders standing dutifully behind. Money had changed hands.

Her gaze pinned Kumarin. "Oh, shut up. For a punch in the mouth? And knowing I'll testify you jumped him first? Forget it."

She pointed at Sanders as he started to speak. "And don't you start. No paperwork's been served. Until you can produce something official, stay out of my way."

As Barney went by, supporting the dazed prisoner, she reached out and stopped him. "Change of plans. Take him to the office and cuff him to a chair. The one bolted to the floor. I want to talk to him later and don't want to have to chase him down. Between you and Agnes, you might get some information out of him. I want to know who he is, where he's from, and especially—who sent him." She stood, hands on hips, watching as chaos returned to order and the music started back up.

She turned and saw Kumarin watching the deputy and prisoner leave the circus called a barn dance. Sighing and watching him carefully, she stepped up to him. As she met his gaze, she shivered. Why she let the man dance with her, she'd never know. His eyes were cold and as appealing as a sunbaked carp three days dead.

"Mr. Kumarin, don't take this the wrong way, but I want you out of my county. Hell, let's back that up a bit. I don't care how you take it. Gather your little army and take them with you. I suggest you leave now."

The man feigned a hurt expression. "I thought we were friends. You may not realize it, but I have a lot to offer."

"You have nothing to offer...never did." She paused a moment. "Look, I gave you a dance and may have given you the wrong impression. If that's the case, I apologize. Just be clear about this. I'm not your friend. I will never be your friend. And unlike certain people in this town, you can't buy me."

She'd returned her pistol to her belt and at the look on his face, kept her hand on the grip. "I think I've made myself clear, Mr. Kumarin."

He stared at her a moment and then looked around at the people who stared back at him. His expression was mocking. "As you wish. I'll step aside for a while. Sorry we couldn't be friends. And for your information, everyone has a price—everyone. I just have to find it." He turned to go, with his new-bought sheriff in tow, and then stopped.

"Acting Sheriff Morris, you'll have your papers Monday morning." He didn't smile but stared at her a moment. "By that time, I'll own the new sheriff, the local highway patrol, and a good part of your board of commissioners. Then we'll see who leaves."

Too many questions were unanswered, and like most law enforcement, she hated a mystery. Nothing made sense. He was buying the town. Why?

"Kumarin." Her voice stopped him and Sanders. "Why all this dog-and-pony show? Your boss said to stop all action, and he didn't strike me as a man to disobey."

She got Sanders to meet her gaze before he returned

to studying the floor. "You're turning good men into criminals just for the lure of money and whatever your agenda is. I don't understand what you get out of it."

Kumarin contemplated her a moment and then smiled. "Well, answering the last part first—because I can. And the first part? I'm old school. It's a matter of honor. Word of something like this will get around—it always does. In our business, we can't allow someone to disrespect us the way he's done. He disrespected Tony in the worst way—he attacked his manhood. It cannot go unpunished. I'm the payback. As for Anton...well, he'll have his own problems soon enough. When he's gone, I'll just step into the vacuum he leaves and take over. Then I'll have it all. But first, this little matter must be taken care of to everyone's satisfaction. People are watching. An organization like ours runs on fear and respect. You must know that."

He rubbed his jaw. "Besides, he made it personal."

"If you take one step out of line, Kumarin, I'll be waiting."

He shrugged but lost his smile. "An empty threat. Monday, Miss Acting Sheriff. You'll have your legal paperwork then. After that, who knows? Maybe I'll come and visit you. We know where you live. We know where everyone lives."

Having watched the man in action for a short amount of time, she had no doubt of his capabilities. "Who will sign the papers? You or the judge?"

He laughed. "By then there won't be any difference." Kumarin walked out into the night followed by her troubled gaze.

This was crazy. Kumarin had just given her a lot of information—said it right out in the open. That meant he thought she didn't matter, that she couldn't do anything about it. He could be right.

She stayed another half hour and was about to leave for Springfield to check on Jim when a voice called out to her. She turned and saw the medic that was attending to Jim in the ambulance.

"Dave, I thought you'd be halfway to Springfield by now."

The man pushed his fingers through his long hair. "Nope. He signed a waiver and left on his own volition. We just pulled around to the back of the parking lot."

Guilt crept into her mind again. But she felt her action was the right decision. Once the knife-wielding attacker had dropped his knife, it was no longer self-defense. She was afraid Jim would kill the man. It took her a moment to get away from Kumarin. Full of adrenaline, she'd pulled her sidearm and hit Jim with it—too hard. The look he gave her as he went down—she'd carry that to her grave.

She tried to keep the tremor from her voice. "Was he okay?"

"Depends on your definition. Was he walking? Yeah, he was. He wasn't tracking too well. Anyway, he got in his truck and left. I'd guess he's home by now."

She never knew worry could hit her so hard—hadn't felt it since before her husband died. "Or maybe he's piled up in a ditch somewhere." She headed toward the door. "Dammit, you should have told me he did that."

"Look, I don't have to let—" His portable radio went nuts with different people talking at once and overriding conversation.

EIGHTEEN

THE MEDIC KEYED HIS RADIO.

"Wayne, what's going on?" They barely heard over the chatter, "—*someone seen running from the sheriff's office—no answer at 9-1-1, so calls are rolling over to the closest county.*"

All the EMS used the same county-wide frequency. Outlying patrol cars were calling in to check on the problem. Surrounding counties call centers were tying up the airwaves trying to find out information. Most were calling White Rock PD and not getting answers.

Rita was out the door, into her Jeep, and peeling out inside of a minute. When she skidded into the parking lot of the sheriff's office ten minutes later, she noted the only extra car was a highway patrol cruiser. She raced up the steps and into a nightmare.

The main floor of the building was open concept with a large main area and then cubicles of offices toward the back. Everything could be seen from the door going in.

For a moment, she thought she'd throw up. People

were down. Their wounds were so obvious she didn't give any thought to rushing up to them right away. Agnes was staring at her with sightless eyes. Rita could almost hear her saying to put on her big girl panties and take care of business. She turned away a moment, squeezing her eyes so hard she was sure there'd be bruising.

Get it together. Get it together now.

Three people gone and two of them friends. Taking a deep breath to calm herself and wishing she hadn't because of the smell, she whirled on the patrolman and grabbed him by the arm.

"Did you clear the area? Do we have an active shooter?"

Patrolman Bob Detwiler stood just inside the door where he'd tried to bar her entry. "There was nobody here when I arrived. You should stay out. This is a crime scene, Rita."

"You just got here?" When he didn't answer, she hit him with another question. "Did you clear the rooms in back?"

He didn't answer.

"What about county-wide? Did you make the double-nuts call?"

The universal call no one ever wants to make. Officer down—converge on scene. At his blank look, she grabbed his handheld off his shoulder, switched to a common frequency that would go to every law enforcement in radio distance.

"This is Limestone County. Clear the channel! I repeat, clear the channel for Limestone County."

She waited a moment while she heard the neighboring counties repeat the clear channel request and hoped her voice didn't go over as shrill as it sounded to her.

A hard knot formed in her chest like a bubble about to burst. Agnes was dead.

Her face felt stiff as she tried to hold back tears. She kept her eyes on the cubicles in the back—the only place anyone could be hidden. Within a few seconds, there was nothing coming from the speakers but a faint hiss. It took everything she had to steel herself for the next words.

"This is Limestone County. We have a ten zero-zero, I repeat a ten zero-zero at the office. All units within ten miles converge."

She paused to take a breath and let that sink in. And, since there were no suspects yet, or people to look out for...

"BOLO is negative—outlying units check and record anyone leaving the area. Limestone County is clear."

The radio erupted in chatter. They wouldn't stay away and she didn't blame them. She knew they'd be flocking in from everywhere. She switched channels and made one more call from the patrolman's radio. For once she was glad the local police department had different offices.

"White Rock PD, converge on the south side and clear the building. Do not enter the main room. Three twenty-five and State will hold the front. Also clear the church next door and surrounding buildings."

Her gut feeling was that whoever did this was long gone, or they'd have taken rounds as they arrived. She looked at Detwiler, remembering the scene in the county commissioner's office. Kumarin's bought and paid for patrolman was looking a little green and scared. Maybe reality was sinking in.

She could hear the ambulance pulling in behind her, lights on and siren blaring. When it shut off, the silence was so complete her normal voice sounded like she was shouting.

It took her a moment to respond to the patrolman's comment from what seemed to be a lifetime ago. "I'm not sure you know what a crime scene is, Bob. You stay the hell out of my way."

She spoke to the two medics rushing up to the door, bags in hand. "Stop, guys. You can't help in here. Look, I know it's not your job, but check around outside and keep the looky-loos away until more help comes. Keep everyone out of the parking lot."

She looked the patrolman in the eye. "Bob would help you with that, but his feet seem to be nailed to the floor."

She could hear shouts from the back of the building as they cleared the rooms. The rear area flooded with police and first responders—a good part of the citizenry was volunteer sheriff's patrol, armed and damned dangerous.

Rita prayed for no shooting because there were some pissed off and scared people out there. If shooting started, they'd kill themselves in the crossfire. A terrible thought hit her—she wouldn't get a chance to notify family. She was sure the word was already out.

Agnes had a husband and family, and Barney's girlfriend usually brought him a sandwich about now. She tried to stomp the hurt back down, and it was damned hard to do. Pulling on her experience in the military, she started to calm down. Except...Agnes. Her mother confessor—was gone.

After a few deep breaths, she advanced into the room

and started taking pictures with her smartphone, including a picture of Detwiler standing by the front door. This wasn't standard protocol, but nothing was standard about this mess.

She turned on the video function and walked to Agnes, speaking as she went.

"We have three victims. All of them are dead. Agnes has a single gunshot to the side of her head. Looks small caliber. There is an exit wound, so we need to find that slug. Her hand is in her purse. It looks like she was going for her pistol. She must have seen something. Her headset is on the desk, and as far as I know, no call went out."

She bent to look, using the camera. "Her sidearm is still in her handbag." She took a deep breath and laid a gentle hand on the dead woman's shoulder one last time and hoped the forensics people wouldn't find the tear that dropped on the purse. Shaking her head hard, she squeezed her eyes shut again. She needed to cry...to break down and let go—and knew she couldn't. It startled her, but she wanted Jim.

Dammit, Agnes. What happened?

She walked over to the chair a few feet away, careful where she stepped and still recording.

"Barney is dead, with a single gunshot wound to the back of his head. His weapon is in its holster. It doesn't look like he saw it coming."

Her recording would show her checking the carotid of each victim, although it was unnecessary.

"The man he brought in for questioning is dead from a single gunshot wound to his forehead. He has prison tats, so I'm thinking an ID will be quick. From the looks of the wound, again small caliber—maybe a twenty-two. No exit wounds from these two men."

She paused, looking around. "It appears to me someone walked in the door as Barney was cuffing the suspect to the chair. He would have had his back to the door. One shot to him since he had the only visible firearm. The next shot to Agnes, off to the side. And the last shot to the prisoner since he was restrained. This was a quick in-and-out operation. I'm guessing it took a minute. Maybe less. Three shots and a very good shooter."

She finished with the video by scanning the room and showing men and women standing in the cubicle area waiting for more instructions. Guns were drawn, pointing at the floor. Shaking her head, she waved them back out.

Her voice was sharp when she turned toward the door. "Detwiler."

She put the phone in her front pocket with the lens showing and pointing out, still recording.

"Have someone take prints from the prisoner sitting in the chair. When you get his ID, we'll be a long way toward knowing who did this. Someone didn't want him to talk."

The patrolman hadn't moved from his spot by the door. "We'll take care of it. My people and the new sheriff are fifteen minutes out."

"Fifteen minutes out? Your new-bought sheriff was standing right by me a minute before we found out. Where the hell did he go?"

Detwiler continued as if not interrupted. "I'm thinking it was your buddy. From what I hear, Lane already tried to kill the man in the chair when he was at the dance. I'm betting he came back to finish the job."

Rita took a deep breath. A faint smell of cordite filled the air, and one of the victims had voided.

"Don't be an idiot. Look around you. This was a professional job. One round forward for Barney and then left for Agnes. The last shot for the prisoner. If someone hadn't been reported running away, this would be a cold scene.

"This is a residential neighborhood. I'm betting you won't interview anyone who heard shots fired. So, if you want another educated guess? They used a suppressor. If not a professional weapon, it was damned specialized."

She put her hand on his shoulder and he flinched away, not meeting her gaze.

"Bob, no matter what's gone on before, money changing hands, intimidation—whatever. That's all out the window. This trumps everything. State will have the lead on this one. Run your own investigation. Jim Lane didn't do this, and you know it. He carries a forty-caliber Glock, just like mine and probably yours. That's a fact. He'd shoot in self-defense, but not—this."

She looked around her one more time. Nothing more to do but bury the dead. She wanted to stay, but knew she'd never be allowed to investigate her own department no matter the circumstances.

"Okay. I'm out. It's all yours. Make your calls and take care of business. I'm going to check on Lane." It took another deep breath to calm her nerves. "Bob, when I broke up that fight tonight, I hit him too hard. The medic shouldn't have released him and mentioned Jim wasn't tracking too well. I don't think he could physically do this."

One more time she looked at the bodies, still recording with her phone. "Bob, be sure to look for brass. I'm betting they cleaned up the area."

"Or used a revolver." His voice sounded hollow in the quiet room.

"Yeah, that too." She thought of Spock in the old *Star Trek* series. Possibilities were endless.

Thinking of that made her feel old. God, what a mess.

Outside, she leaned against her Jeep, holding her head against the cool metal. She sucked the night air deep into her lungs—ignoring questions from the gathering crowd. After twenty years in the military, she should be used to this. A sob broke through before she could stop it.

Agnes. I'm sorry.

She got into her vehicle and sat hugging herself. She couldn't stop the racking sobs that broke through her resolve to be strong. It took a few minutes, but she finally stopped. Blowing her nose didn't help her sore throat or answer any questions. What in the hell was going on? She raised her head and looked across the parking lot to see Kumarin standing under a streetlight at the edge of the growing crowd, staring at her. As she watched, he disappeared into the darkness. The connection was obvious, at least to her.

Russian. And he didn't care who knew because they couldn't prove it.

And where was the new sheriff? He'd left the dance hall with Kumarin.

Her head swirled with disjointed snippets of information all pointing in one direction.

Sonofabitch!

———

JIM STOOD on his front porch enjoying the night air. The cooling breeze brought the scent of pine from the surrounding trees. The honeysuckle hedge filled the air with its cloying odor—a smell too sweet to be fragrant.

It was amazing how just a few days ago he was content. Dumb, misinformed to a certain extent...but happy. What was the old saying? Circumstances alter circumstances.

He leaned against the porch's support post for a moment, deciding where to go. Going camping wasn't on the top of his list of things to do, but he couldn't defend the cabin. Not against what he felt was coming. You must be alive to fight back, which is rule number one in any conflict. The Russians would be ruthless, and for whatever reasons they had, he was in their crosshairs. Most people would run to town for the protection of the law. That wasn't his way, and it was more than being more comfortable and feeling safer in the woods.

Law enforcement can't protect you 24/7, and they all have families. He had respected and supported their mantra—I'm going home to my family tonight, regardless of what I have to do today.

With that in mind, a deputy or patrolman might hesitate at that critical moment when they risked their lives to protect him, endangering both in the process—unintended consequences. He had too much respect to put them in that position. Law enforcement's job was dangerous enough. And as much as he was disappointed in her, he couldn't think of putting Rita or any of her staff in that position.

When he first came to this place, he'd used physical

labor to heal himself. It took a lot of labor. His walking trails and a couple of footbridges were a testament of that, including his terraced gardens going down to the lake.

On one of his excursions, and about a mile from the cabin, he'd found the remains of a hunter's camp. It was old and abandoned, built in a shallow cave surrounded by a wild growth of grapevine and scrub brush. The foliage walled it up in the front, making a snug sanctuary against cool nights. He'd replaced the wooden wall and door with pressure-treated lumber and destroyed any outward sign of man, including a fire pit. Nature reclaimed the rest and made it invisible from just a few feet away.

He visited the hideaway on occasion to stock it with dried or preserved meals and water. It was an old habit giving him a sanctuary to escape to in case things got bad —a prepper's paradise.

He came alert to his surroundings when he heard them coming, not so much by the sound of the engines but by the whine of tires on the blacktop road. As he glanced toward the highway, he saw headlights go out, but the noise of their tires on blacktop kept going. That alone spelled trouble.

One vehicle stopped short of his drive and another went past to stop beyond the turnoff. He knew the occupants of those vehicles would be coming on foot as a flanking movement to box him in. A third vehicle started down his lane and then stopped. He wondered how they could see. The moon wasn't up and the night was dark as an inkwell. No matter. It was time to go.

He hit the ground running, moving to his left toward the walking trail. And fell sprawling. He got up and moved at a slower pace toward the trail, fighting through dizziness. The sound of his breathing shut out all other sounds. When he stopped to listen, the swishing of weeds on pant legs and crackle of bodies forcing through brush gave away the positions of the men advancing toward his cabin. They weren't trying to be quiet, confident in their numbers.

He kept pushing himself until he thought his position was outside their line of attack and then slowed again to listen. A motor started and the sound moved down the lane. He realized they'd been waiting for everyone to get into position before the last vehicle started up. That meant they had communication. If they were that sophisticated, they'd have night-vision apparatus. The occupants of the last vehicle were going toward his house. The point of the spear. Military or mercenaries? In that moment he knew the whole screwed-up situation had progressed far beyond a couple of wannabe bad guys from the big city.

As he walked away, he heard shooting and he stopped again. He'd put a lot of work in that house, and now they were blowing out the windows and punching it full of holes. From the sound, their fusillade was all small caliber.

He hoped they'd catch themselves in their own crossfire. When he heard a muffled thump, he realized they'd thrown a flash or smoke device into his home and would follow with their assault on the interior. That's the way he'd have done it—shock and awe while keeping the invading force safe and opponent pinned down.

The shotgun came unbidden to his hands as he took a step back toward the house. Now would be an excellent time for an assault of his own. They'd be distracted and not watching their back. His finger caressed the trigger guard on the shotgun and then dropped away. If he attacked and then had to run, he wouldn't make it. His body wouldn't allow it.

But his time would come. Soon.

NINETEEN

HE WALKED along the path until he came near the place to leave the trail. The moon was coming up and he could see a little, but he'd need to wait until morning to finish his trip. He walked off the trail and up the incline, chancing for a moment to use his small flashlight.

His head pounded and his strength was fading. He'd pushed as far as possible—he couldn't go any farther. Especially stumbling around in the dark. He'd put a good distance between him and whoever attacked his house. It would be a surprise if they came looking for him. Whoever they were seemed good at attacking a building, but he doubted they wanted to search the forest. They'd be smart enough to put out spotters, but he'd worry about that tomorrow.

There was a thick copse of sumac and brush in front of him. Crawling in, he reached into his pack and brought out a black Mylar survival blanket. Although the thin material was noisy to spread out, it would keep him warm. If they were following him with night-sensor or heat-sensing goggles? Good luck with that. He rolled up in the blanket and tried to sleep. Just him and the ants. And whatever scurried away when he crawled in.

———

ALINA SAT on a plush sofa with her feet up on a padded footstool. She'd never seen her father this angry, and there weren't a dozen people who could tell it by looking at him. It was a rare day when he showed any kind of emotion.

After the meeting with Jim Lane, they'd returned to the hotel and purchased a room so Anton could keep a closer watch on the situation unfolding in White Rock.

"This is madness." Anton paced the floor, shaking his head. "I can see taking out The Shank, but the dispatcher and deputy? Stupid! The last thing we need is to stir up these rednecks and draw attention to ourselves."

Gregory brought him a drink from the wet bar. "Our people say it's contained, so far. Viktor is spreading money around."

"It won't be." Anton paused to take a drink. "You can't smooth something like that over. There is not that much money." He whirled and pointed at Alina. "This is your fault."

She shook her head and replied with more calmness than she felt. "I contributed...maybe. If it weren't for Tony, none of this would be going on."

Shaking his head, Anton asked, "Where is Tony?"

Alina glanced at Gregory before answering. "When we came back to the hotel, he'd already left with someone. He's in the wind, so to speak."

Anton shook his head. "In the wind. That bastard better be on a sailboat to China."

"You want us to find him?" Gregory settled onto the other end of the sofa from Alina.

The mob boss stopped pacing a moment, lost in thought. "No. I got a good idea where he is." He looked at them. "I want this cleaned up. Now." His hard gaze pinned Gregory. "No more assets or funds. Shut it down. All Tony and Viktor have with them now are a bunch of lightweights. We can't control what's already there, but anything else is not happening."

He turned to Alina. "Can Viktor get him? Lane? He'd have to kill that lady cop too."

She was slow to answer. "With a dozen men? Maybe. They're amateurs, all except Viktor, but you never know. Mistakes happen. I researched him, but most of his record is a big blank. Same as you found. My gut says no, but..."

Anton nodded, watching her closely. "He got to you, didn't he? I warned against using him for cover."

"Yeah, Pops. He got to me. He's one of the good guys." She watched her father standing before her. He seemed to lose focus for a moment and then his face settled into hard lines.

"I have to get back to St. Louis. As you know, the Feds are crawling out my nose and into my ears. My sources say I'll be arrested when I get back." He shrugged. "Again."

His gaze settled on her. "You're in charge until I make bail. Our lawyers are already primed and ready to go. But you clean up this mess. Use Gregory. Can you do what needs to be done? They've stepped all over us. Viktor wants to be head of the family business, and Tony has caused more grief than he's worth. I want them to disappear. People are watching to see what we do—how we handle it. They're always watching. We don't need this. I'm counting on you, Alina."

She glanced at Gregory's deadpan expression and then at her father's. If Viktor's minions killed Jim, it would be her pleasure to take care of it. Hell, it would be her pleasure either way.

"As you wish."

TWENTY

RITA WAS SLOWING down to turn into Jim's drive when her headlights caught a vehicle going away around the bend ahead of her. Her fleeting glimpse made her think it was a dark SUV. That thought took her to the vehicles the Russians were driving. What are they doing out here? Her mind came out of the fog brought on by the murder of her friends and her unofficial firing from her job.

She ticked off bullet points from the checklist in her mind. Russian mob. Kumarin. A man tried to knife Jim tonight.

Shit.

She sped down the lane and skidded to a stop in front of the cabin. The headlights turned the scene into a surreal painting as she looked at the house. The windows were all smashed and the front door hung by one hinge. Pockmarks adorned the wood sides next to the windows and door. She pulled her sidearm and walked through the door into the living room. Her shoes crunched on glass and she froze. The house felt empty, but she needed to clear it. They might have left someone behind, but she doubted that. Thinking of the vehicle she noticed leaving, hit and run seemed more their style.

Backing up, her hand found the light switch and flipped it up. Nothing. She wasn't one that liked to go through a dark house with a flashlight like on the television shows. That would tell the bad guys *her* location, not theirs. If memory served, there was a utility room in the back and she went to that. Her penlight showed the main breaker was off. Taking a deep, calming breath, she switched it on.

The house was in shambles. Her first irrational thought was that she was tired of straightening this place up. Hell, she had her own place to tidy up, if she felt the urge. Checking all the rooms and looking around outside, she found nothing. Not finding anyone was a relief—not finding Jim made her chest ache.

His truck was here but he wasn't. Whatever happened, she had to trust that he got away. Otherwise, there was no other reason for trashing the place in anger.

She wouldn't try to find him in the dark. Staying in the house was a low risk for now. She had no doubt she could hear any vehicles approaching. Cleaning would give her something to do, so she set to the task. After an hour of work, the place looked halfway presentable. At least she'd swept up the glass and thrown it away. She decided to keep a light on just in the room she cleaned to cut down on bugs.

Finding the window in the bedroom still intact, she closed the door and drew the shades. It surprised her that they were blackout curtains. She turned on the light. The recliner looked inviting. Tired, she sank into its comfort. A tee shirt lay across one arm of the chair. She held it to her nose for a moment and then clutched it to her chest. If this was all she could have tonight, she'd take it.

She thought again that it would be fruitless to try and find Jim in the dark. There were no bloodstains or bodies to be seen, so she felt he was gone when the visitors arrived. She'd just stay here and search in the morning. Chances were that the Russians—and she didn't doubt that for a moment—wouldn't be back. If they did and saw her clearly marked Jeep, with County Sheriff stenciled on the back, they'd most likely leave. Maybe.

Her thoughts turned to Jim. She'd hit him too hard. Dammit, why'd she hit him at all? A man was trying to kill him, for God's sake. There wouldn't be a jury in Limestone County that would convict him of anything.

She looked around the room that was a man cave, thinking it was his area of comfort. There was a gun rack over the door and a couple of antique shotguns nestled there. One part of the room held what military vets called his vanity wall—framed awards and medals, and a State of Missouri boilerplate recognition of service award.

Another wall had a built-in bookshelf filled with Louis L'Amour westerns. She looked closer and saw a couple of volumes of poetry by Burns and Bryant, and a copy of *An Outline of History* by H. G. Wells. Looking at it, she saw a copyright date of 1920.

Huh. He likes old stuff.

Drumming her fingers in boredom on the end table by the chair, she turned her attention to the pull-out drawer and wondered if she should look inside. She'd already looked through his chest of drawers and closet. How many socks and tee shirts does one man need? And hiking boots? This man needed to make a trip to the local

Christian center where people could get clothes for a quarter, and make a serious donation.

With a sigh, and hoping she wasn't a cat and that curiosity wouldn't kill her, she slid open the drawer. Empty. Almost. Laying in the center of the drawer was a business card.

Holding the card up, she saw it was blank on one side and had a number embossed on the other. She held the card by the edges, tapping it against her palm, thinking about what she knew of Jim's past. Not much. But her husband had told her to trust him and hinted at some shadow organization. Not any of the alphabet agencies most people heard about. Something different. Few business cards just had a number. There were enough digits, so she took a chance. Hell, what else did she have to do? She pulled out her cell phone and made the call—again, hoping she wasn't a cat.

The phone rang once and the response was cryptic.

"How did you get this number?" The woman's voice was neither helpful nor antagonistic. Just a simple question that to Rita's mind, spoke volumes. When she didn't answer right away, the question was repeated.

"I'm looking at a business card," she finally replied. Two could play the cryptic game.

There was silence a moment before the voice came back asking the obvious question. "Who gave you the card?"

"Who the hell are you?" This was getting ridiculous and reminded her of trying to keep someone on the line while doing a phone trace.

The neutral voice repeated the question with the same tone and inflection. "Who gave you the card?"

Rita emitted a sigh of the downtrodden and put-upon. "Jim Lane. I'm at his house." A small lie but permissible.

Again, silence. Finally. "Are you in danger?"

"Me? Uh, no. Not right now. At least not that I know of."

What the hell? Why was she so defensive? The dead cat scenario started to loom larger in her mind.

"If anyone is in danger, it's Jim."

"Understood. Someone will call you back, Rita." The voice could have been a robot for all the inflection it gave. Maybe it was... Wait.

Rita?

Her cell rang within a minute. This time it was a different woman. This one cared.

"My name is Sally. Listen to me carefully. I have your name from phone records. We have your location marked with GPS. From your comment, you are in Jim Lane's house. Are you in immediate danger?"

Rita had better answers this time. "Not that I know of, but it's possible."

"Secure your location and call me back." The silence stretched a moment. "Please believe me, Rita. We're on your side. Get safe and then call."

She sat looking at the phone as the call dropped. Okay, now that spooked her. How did they get her phone records and location so fast? Why would they assume she was in danger?

The front door creaked as it swung on its remaining hinge. Wind? Her hand snaked out and switched off the light. She pulled her pistol from her belt and made her way out front. The sound of the voice startled her so much it was a damned good thing she didn't have her finger on the trigger.

"Rita, I know you're in here. Your Jeep's out front."

So much for hearing a vehicle approach. She relaxed. It was acting wannabe Sheriff Ted Sanders. Then her guard went back up. What was he doing here? She stopped before going into the front room, knowing he couldn't see her standing in the shadows. Poor Ted, however, was silhouetted by the outside light that'd come on when she restored power. Not the sharpest knife in the drawer.

"What's up, Ted?"

Using a flashlight, Ted was looking around at the mess. He used his heel to scuff at the black mark left on the hardwood floor. "I thought Lane would be a better housekeeper than this. It's a mess in here." He looked hard at where he supposed her to be. "Why don't you come out here where I can see you?"

"I'm good right here. What do you want?" The phone call with Sally was rubbing off on her. Her answers were short and to the point.

"Look, bad things have happened. We'll get it sorted out." He walked to a shattered window and peered out. "You need to come into town, it's safer there. Being around Lane will get you hurt. We don't want anyone else getting hurt."

She shook her head, even though she knew he couldn't see it. "We? Who's we? Is that what you've been told to say? Has your Russian benefactor told you what this is all about? Why they are after Lane? No? You're aiding and abetting murder, Ted. Right up to your eyeballs. I think it's time you went back to town. For *your* own safety."

"Dammit, you and Johnny always lorded it over me. You wouldn't give me a break for anything. Then when

Johnny died, you still wouldn't give me the time of day."

He turned to look toward her, his face illuminated by the outside light. "Guess the shoe is on the other foot now, huh? We'll see who the big man is around here after this, won't we?"

She held her pistol at her side. He was the one she gave an attitude adjustment to when she took over as chief deputy. He was a coward...but more dangerous because of it. She didn't want this to escalate any further.

"Ted, get out of here. No matter how hard you try, you're all hat and no cattle." He took a step toward her when she stopped him with a question.

"Will you speak at Agnes's funeral? And Barney's? It's your job now. Will you tell their families how you got to be such a big man, as you put it? How you got my job? How people's lives were sacrificed for your pocketbook?" She stepped out into the light, her pistol pointed at his belly. "You're a coward, Ted. You deserve whatever the Russians will give you. Now, leave."

As usual, he didn't argue. He simply stared at her a moment before leaving. As she watched him drive up the lane, she pulled up her cell phone, went to recent calls, and keyed the last number. It connected right away.

"Are you safe?"

"For the moment." She walked back to Jim's bedroom and closed the door. Somehow, she felt safe there.

"Okay. I'll be recording this, just so I don't forget anything. Tell me everything that's happened. Start to finish, rumors and facts. I need all the insignificant little details that you think may not matter. I need everything. Are you lovers?"

Rita about dropped the phone. "What?"

The woman chuckled. "Sorry, I just threw that in there."

Rita laughed with her, glad for the respite, knowing and appreciating how one little comment put them at ease with each other. Considering how much had gone on, the debrief—and that's what it felt like—didn't take long. She wrapped it up in ten minutes.

"So, that's where we are. Jim's running around in the woods with a probable concussion. That's not counting any wounds he may have received when the Russians attacked the house. I'm sitting in his shot-up house waiting for daylight so I can go out and look for him. There's so much going on I can't get a handle on it."

"Well, like they say, buck up, buttercup. It's big girl time and you may have to get mean in a hurry. You need to prepare yourself for that."

Sally laughed. "Okay, clichés aside. It's not surprising he's gone native on you. That's where he's comfortable and most effective. And for damned sure, that's where he's the most dangerous. If you do go looking for him, which I do not recommend at this point, make plenty of noise so he knows you're coming."

The woman paused a moment, and Rita could hear fingernails drumming on a tabletop.

"Don't give up, Rita. You have help now. We're on it. Jim is one of ours and we help our own—whether he wants it or not."

Rita had the distinct feeling she'd lost control of the situation when she called that phone number. "Just what is one of yours? Who are you? What do you do?"

"Not now. That's a story for when we have more time. Face time. You're ex-military, so you'll understand what I'm telling you. Keep your shit wired tight and your head on a swivel. Get yourself safe and him too...if you can. He attracts trouble like flies swarm to honey, so I don't know if you can keep him safe. Just—if you find him—tell him Sally is coming. He'll know."

Ex-military? How'd she know that? She liked this woman, even if they'd only met on the phone. She seemed real, if it wasn't an act.

"I'll do my best. And to answer your first question, we're not lovers. I doubt we ever will be."

"Why? He was always a hottie with a capital H, even on a bad day."

She sighed again, thinking the act was becoming a habit. "I'm the one who hurt him. The look he gave me when he went down—he may never forgive me. I may never forgive myself."

Rita sat on the back deck of Jim's cabin waiting for first light, and grimaced at the taste of the instant coffee she made. She hoped the coffee and the bottle of Dr. Pepper would give her the jolt she needed to stay awake. After her conversation with Sally, sleep wouldn't come. She'd told her to wait until help arrived, but all she could wait for was the first crack of dawn to go look for him.

In the silence and blanket of darkness surrounding her, the events of the preceding days engulfed her. Shit, she thought things were under control. The plan to resign as sheriff and spend her days chasing a certain hunk living in this cabin seemed viable.

Then came the first shooting and the meeting with the Russians—the dance and the knife fight. The fact that she clunked Jim on the head to save a man's life that she couldn't care less about weighed heavy on her mind.

So, you hurt the one you love to save one you don't care about. Pure craziness. How do you square that?

And when had the L word come about?

She took another shot of the bitter brew and felt close to tears. Again. There were too many questions. Could she have done something to save Agnes and Barney? Why'd she send the prisoner to the office instead of the more secure jail? That act alone got people killed. God, she just wanted to crawl into a hole and die. What could she do to fix it?

Thanks to the Russians spreading a lot of money around, at least she thought that was the case, local law enforcement and the county commission turned against her. They warned her not to interfere. All that so the Russians, or Mafia, or who-ever-the-hell they were, could kill Jim with little or no blowback.

Now help was coming, and she was supposed to wait for them. But Jim was hurt and out there somewhere. That's where she needed to be. Smart or not, she'd be gone at daylight.

TWENTY-ONE

JIM WOKE with a start as a stray slice of filtered sunlight hit his eyes. He stayed motionless for a moment as the events of the last few days danced across his memory. The Mylar blanket crinkled as he sat up and looked around.

He'd gone off trail and dug into a stand of scrub brush and weeds the night before, knowing he couldn't navigate in the darkness. His internal alarm usually got him up before dawn. That failed him today. Now he had to be careful. If the shooters from the night before had staked out any of the trails, they'd see his movement right away.

Listening for sounds that weren't normal, his mind filtered out the birds and insects, along with a squirrel that was irritated about something. Blue jays loved to pick on squirrels. They were always feuding.

When he looked to the east, all he saw were silhouetted trees shrouded in mist with the sunlight peeking through. The air held the lingering scent of wild clematis. And a skunk had passed by in the night. Not through his little hideaway, thank you, God.

Limestone rocks protruded through the undergrowth, covered in green moss and gray lichen. Sunlight crept through the canopy of leaves above. At any other time, he'd be relishing this cloudless morning and the cool, fragrant air. Right now, it was like a bad horror movie. But this was his domain and no place for indecision.

He froze at the sound of leaves rustling and something scraping on a tree limb. Slowly turning his head, he saw a magnificent whitetail buck stepping up the slope about thirty yards away. He waited a few moments and three does followed, along with a couple of fawns.

When they passed by, he shrugged off the survival blanket and rolled to his knees. The presence of the deer told him all he needed to know. They were great sentinels, and he doubted the city boys could fool them.

Folding the metal blanket into a hand-sized pad, he stuffed it into his pack, found his water bottle, and had a long drink. He took his hat off and felt the back of his head. No fresh blood. There'd never been much anyway, and he couldn't feel any swelling. As an experiment, he shook his head vigorously.

Crap!

The world spun, and he found himself leaning forward on his hands. He fought off nausea, thinking of taking the Meclizine in his pack. But the medication would make him drowsy and he couldn't afford that. In a few moments, he felt better and stood.

No more head shaking.

After checking his guns for debris and dirt, he shouldered his pack and started up the hill. It would take an hour to get to the camp, and then he could rest. He had decisions to make. For now, he was too close to his cabin and needed to move.

He stopped just short of the top of the hill. Something walked along the ridge making an inordinate amount of noise. Thinking it would be someone hiking the nature trails, he peeked over the crest and saw Rita coming toward him. He watched with amusement as she kicked leaves as she went and used a wooden walking stick to crack against the small trees. She advanced toward him for a few moments before he spoke.

"You're giving me a headache."

At the first sound of his voice, she flinched backward, holding her hand to her chest. She stood breathing hard for a moment.

"Dammit, Jim. You scared the shit out of me." She gathered herself and walked toward him. "I was making noise so you wouldn't think I was sneaking up on you and shoot me."

"Stop." When she froze, he stood, listening and watching back the way she'd come. He spoke in a near whisper. "For the record...I don't shoot what I can't see." He took his hat off and rubbed his head. "What do you want, Rita? Come to finish the job?"

At her crushed expression, he regretted saying it but let the comment hang out there. It was a question that needed answering.

She used the back of her hand to wipe away a tear, and he could see her eyes starting to flood. Her bottom lip quivered before she got it under control. "I came to find you and make sure you're all right."

With a shrug and long sigh, she turned and started away. "I guess you are."

Lately, indecision seemed to be a shirt he wore every day, especially concerning Rita. Everything she did affected him in some way and he wasn't sure he liked that. But she deserved to have her say.

"Hey." She stopped walking and turned to look at him with tears coursing their way down her cheeks. He stared at the tears a moment, thinking of an old Simon and Garfunkel lullaby called "Kathy's Song."

"Look, I'm sorry. You didn't deserve that." He smiled a little. "Well, maybe a little bit. We can talk at the camp." When she started to say something, he held his finger to his lips. "Not now. I seem to be short on energy this morning. Will you come with me?"

She nodded, wiping a hand across her cheeks.

Another hour of hiking found them halfway down the side of a steep hill. He was embarrassed that twice she'd helped him when he stumbled. They stood on a huge outcropping of limestone that overlooked a large part of the lake. He pointed to the moss on the shady side of the flat-topped rock.

"Don't step on that. You'll leave tracks and it's slick."

There were stepping stones that went around the side of the rock that appeared natural, but someone laid them long ago. Grass grew between the stones along with taller weeds. The circular path brought them out below the rock to a flat area about fifty feet across. One step past the clearing involved a sheer drop to the rocky shore of the lake below.

He put his pack down against the rock, and she moved to join him.

"You look worn out, Jim. You'd better sit." She moved her pack around, took his arm, and helped him sit with his back to the rock. It was shady and cool, but he was sweating from the exertion.

Rummaging around in a side pocket of her pack, she

came up with a bottle of water and a container of pills. "Take one of these."

"What's this?"

She rattled the bottle. "I knew you might be a little woozy, so I have Meclizine for that. After I whacked you on the head, I thought you might need it."

"What are you, a walking pharmacy?" He shook his head in slow motion. "That'll make me sleepy. I'd rather have something for the headache."

"Well, let's see. Headache? Dizziness? Nausea?" He nodded at each one. "Well, you flunked that test. No painkillers for you, at least not for a while."

She then started to cry and put her head on his shoulder, hands rubbing his chest. "I'm so sorry I hit you. I was excited and afraid you'd kill him and go to jail..."

"Will you stop blubbering?" He smiled to take the sting from his words, his hand tracing the tears down to her mouth, silencing her. "We need to make camp."

"Well, since we're so busy, I guess I'll apologize later." She stood, giving him a curious glance, hands on hips, as she looked around. "Where are we making camp? Right here? Okay. We can move this..."

He moved to the other end of the rock and pulled away some vines. She watched with her mouth open as he opened a weathered wooden door. The green mold on the front let it blend in with the vines surrounding it.

"Well, I'll be damned." Her voice was low and throaty.

"Let's hope not." He reached inside and pulled out a battery-powered lantern and separate batteries encased in a plastic bag. Installing the batteries, he turned on the light and gave it to her. While she held it, they went inside. He took her walking stick and began poking into corners.

"There may be snakes, usually a copperhead. Sometimes they wander in." He paused and sniffed the air. "I don't smell one, though. And they always flunk the smell test."

She shuddered so hard the beam of the light wiggled on the floor. "Snakes don't wander. They slither."

Pointing to the walls, he continued. "The walls are so smooth, there's not much way for them to climb. If they're not on the floor, we should be okay."

"I don't like snakes." She started to back out of the space.

He reached out and grabbed her shirt. "Get back in here, you coward. Look, I'm going to rest, so you need to keep watch. There's a fire extinguisher right over there. If you happen to see something slithering around, as you say, just spray it and then toss it out or kill it. Personally, I prefer dead copperheads and timber rattlers, but it's your choice."

"Rattlers?" She waved the light around the floor. "Can we leave the light on?"

"Suit yourself." Setting the lantern on end, pointing at the rock ceiling, he picked a large, plastic-wrapped bundle off a rock shelf and took out a rubberized ground sheet. After he spread it over the floor, he snagged a sleeping bag from another spot and rolled it out. Lying down, he used his pack for a pillow.

Before he drifted away, he heard her sigh and sit next to him—felt her hand on his side. He flinched when she hit the cut on his side, causing a flurry of apologies. Finally, with her hand in his hair, he relaxed, knowing she would keep watch and wondering where the trust came from. After all, she hit him...

———

HE SLEPT with restless dreams and vivid memories marching through his mind—gun battles and an innocent mother and child needing rescue, knife fights, and Tony One-Ball. Somewhere in his dreaming, he felt comforted by arms around him and whispering in his ear.

A short scream and whooshing sound propelled him from sleep. The cave filled with white smoke. Rolling to his knees, he palmed his gun and pointed it toward the door.

His sight picture found a startled Rita holding the fire extinguisher and staring back at him. Her tousled hair was sticking out, and she had a wild look in her eyes.

He coughed and sneezed. "Open the door and let the fog out. We'll breathe better."

She nodded once and opened the door. From the daylight streaming in, he guessed it was close to noon. He'd slept a long time. The white cloud from the extinguisher began to dissipate. His prayer was that no one would see it.

"Where is it? Did you get it?" At her blank look, he tried again. "The snake? Did you get it?" It was hard to tell in the dim light, but he thought she blushed.

"Uh, no. Not exactly."

He stood and was surprised his head didn't hurt. "Did it get away?"

She wouldn't meet his gaze. "Yes, it ran away."

With his mind a little groggy, he knew he sounded slow on the uptake. "Ran away? Not slithered?"

Her sigh was long and deep, and her shoulders slumped. "All right, dammit. It was a rat." Her expression was defiant. "A big rat. I'm talking terrier-size rat. Big teeth."

He pinched the bridge of his nose between his fingers and took a deep breath.

She stood holding the red extinguisher bottle in front of her. Her voice stuttered. "You...would you...please put down your gun?"

He had to laugh for a moment, holstering his pistol. "You do realize that furry rodents aren't affected much by a cold blast of air?"

Her grin matched his. "I scared the shit out of it. You can see it right over there."

"Yeah, well, you can clean it up." He walked out the door. The day was bright and warm with a cool breeze off the lake. She came to stand beside him and leaned her head on his shoulder. She did the same yesterday, but he was starting to like it.

"Can you forgive me? Please? For all I've done? I'm dying inside."

"You mean like a blanket pardon? For everything? Knocking me senseless? Flocking a rat like a Christmas tree? Making nice to the Russian mob? What?"

Her forehead banged a couple of times against his chest. "I guess you can take your pick. I'm not having a good week. Look. About the Russian. It was stupid. I thought I could get some information from him if he loosened up and enjoyed himself. Nancy Drew, I'm not. I was wrong, and my skin still crawls when I think of dancing with him." She smiled at him. "How about a blanket pardon? Then I won't have to confess so much?"

Hell, what could he do? From this point forward, he felt this was his lady. He just hoped she felt the same. His hand came up to caress her hair as he pulled her closer to him. "Already done. I'm not saying we don't have some issues to work out, but I guess you were doing what you thought was right, although I may never turn my back on you again."

She elbowed him in the ribs. "You already did. And after last night, I feel like I took a beating too. Do you realize you slept through the night? I was afraid you were hurt worse than I thought and would have to drag you out to the hospital."

"That was you holding me? It wasn't a dream?"

"No dream. You were fighting some damned hard battles last night. I'm glad your head is clear today. We need to talk about some things."

He looked at her a moment, feeling the ageless fear of when a woman says we need to talk. To make it worse, he couldn't remember anything from the night before. His voice was wary.

"What things?"

Her smile made him nervous. "Like what you did to me last night. It makes me blush to think about it. I thought I'd seen it all. Boy, was I wrong."

He stared at her while searching his mind. Cohesive thought was a coward sneaking out the back door. He decided bluffing was the proper response.

"Liar."

She stared at him, nodding. Her gaze and expression were a showcase of the wronged.

His response was weak. "No..."

She laughed at his expression. "Gotcha! Yeah, I'm lying. You weren't up to it. Besides, you gave me that courtesy when I was drunk, not taking advantage. I'm paying it forward."

"Jesus, woman." He smiled at her. "I don't know if I should feel relief or disappointment."

He'd been hearing a steady drone for a few moments, but it didn't get his full attention until he heard the engine's throttle back and realized the sound was an airplane. As they watched, a twin-engine turboprop drifted by, right to left in their vision and close to shore. The plane had pontoons along with retracted wheels, possibly a Viking Otter. He hadn't seen one of those in quite a while and only one person he knew favored them because you could pretty much land anywhere. You could land on seventy percent of the water in the world but only about one percent of land. Handy.

He turned to Rita. "I'm starved. There are some dried packages of food inside on the shelf. Pick your poison and I'll get the camp stove going and water boiling."

Four packages of noodles and a couple of tins of mystery meat later, he felt ready. Sort of. When he sat down, she came and sat next to him, touching from shoulder to knee. It felt right.

"So what do we need to discuss? Should we talk about you playing grab-ass with your Russian friend? Or, how about you whacking me on the head? Letting a killer get away—or did he? What's going on, Rita?"

"Well, basically Limestone County is FUBARed." She told him everything, from the time he came in the door at the dance until she left the sheriff's office. She cried again when the story came to Agnes.

He didn't tell her he suspected she'd taken a payoff

like the rest. Let her reputation stay intact. People would miss her. He didn't know Barney very well but knew what a double killing could do to a small town. There'd be a whole bunch of mad and trigger-happy folks around.

"There's one other thing." Her gaze was watchful. "I talked to a woman named Sally and laid it all out for her. Everything I knew. She said to tell you she's coming and don't do anything stupid."

He sighed. "Why on earth did you do that?"

Another thought occurred to him. "How did you do that?"

"There was a card with a number on it. I saw it in your nightstand—got curious and called the number. I took a chance."

She wrung her hands and watched his expression. He thought she looked like the weight of the world sat on her shoulders. "Dammit, I'm responsible for all this. If I hadn't told Barney to take that guy to the office, they might still be alive. If I'd just let you kill that bastard, we wouldn't be in this mess."

Glancing up at him from studying her hands, she continued. "Well, you might be. I don't think the self-defense angle would work. But then again, this is Lime-stone County, and he did attack you first. I swear I need to get out of the decision-making business. I'm piling one bad decision on top of another."

They'd both stood during this last exchange and he pulled her into his arms. Her hair nestled under his chin. "The only people responsible for those murders are the one who pulled the trigger and whoever told him to do it. I think we both have a good idea who that is."

He pushed her away just a little. "Was that the only bad decision?"

"You know it wasn't. Like I said before, I danced with that slimeball. How I let him get that close to me, I'll never know. Hell, I wasn't even drunk. I don't have any kind of excuse that holds water. I tried to get information from him and couldn't pull it off."

"All right. We've got a lot in front of us. It wasn't too long ago you were pushing me away. Where do you stand on that?"

She didn't hesitate. "I'm going to stand as close to you as I can. Thick or thin. Whatever it takes. If that's okay with you?"

He pulled her to him. "Sounds like a proposal. Are you asking?"

"It kinda does, doesn't it? In this new age we live in, I do get to ask. But don't make any rash decisions until you're over your concussion."

He smiled and then kissed her. "Fair enough. I can live with it. Now, let's put everything away and go see Sally."

Rita looked startled. "She's here? How can you know that?"

"Who do you think came in on that seaplane? Santa Claus?"

———

VIKTOR KUMARIN STOOD at the memorial in front of the Limestone County courthouse, hands clasped behind his back and deep in thought, appearing to peruse names he didn't know—or desire to. No matter what country was involved, it was always the same. The poor and needy filled the ranks and were sent off to war, occasionally led by officers looking for fame. They were lured by the love of country and sent to distant shores for obscure reasons by people who cared nothing for them. Politicians were the same the world over. The real movers and shakers were those who controlled the politicians and their narrative. That was the only power that counted in the world.

A black SUV parked diagonally next to him and he watched Tony get out. Tony One-Ball. Viktor chuckled. Americans had a great knack for nicknames.

He chuckled again as Tony cursed, having to jump aside to avoid a collision with a skateboarding teenager. The kid had a cell phone in one hand and cigarette in the other, navigating the sidewalks with practiced ease.

"So, Tony." He tried to keep his distaste from showing. "What brings you out of hiding?"

The man stared at the receding delinquent with distaste, finally turning to address Kumarin. "Trying to clean up your mess. Why isn't this over? You promised me Lane's head on a platter. I don't seem to have it now."

Viktor looked at the smaller man, not trying to hide his contempt anymore. "Things are progressing, both here and at home. Like cogs in a wheel, each must wait its turn. Lane keeps returning to his cabin, thinking we don't want a confrontation out in the forest. I have people coming in that specialize in this." He turned his pale eyes on Tony. "I'll have him and his bitch sheriff very soon."

Tony didn't flinch from his gaze. "Well, don't count on anyone coming. Gregory showed up and offered to help clean up the mess. He also told me no more funds, no more people. What we have on scene is it. Anton is pissed beyond words."

Viktor snorted and then shrugged his dismissal. "Anton is about to be a guest of the state. My people have leaked enough information to send him away a long time. This will be over soon. Do not interfere."

Tony looked at him a moment, unconsciously rubbing his crotch. "Make sure your arrogance doesn't cost you— or us. Lane is tougher than we thought."

"Arrogance and confidence are earned. I have never lost. I won't now. The men I have with me aren't the best, but we'll make do. Lane will be hunted down and killed like his dog. And I will do it."

TWENTY-TWO

BEFORE THEY LEFT THE CAMP, Jim pulled the wild grapevines back to cover the old wooden door and took a final look around the area. It all looked natural except for the two logs they'd sat on. He rolled those to the edge of the clearing by some other wood from a deadfall, being careful the damp side remained on the ground. A log with a wet spot on top of it would be a dead giveaway. The bark on the logs didn't match, but he didn't think anyone would notice. He then scuffed the dirt where the logs had rested, smoothing it out.

"Are we going back the way we came?" While Rita waited, her walking stick was busy poking around bushes and logs.

He watched her for a moment with a smile, finally shaking his head. He couldn't resist. "You know, most things won't bother you if you don't poke them with a stick. And to answer your question, we'll take a different route. Someone could have spotted our first set of tracks and set up an ambush in case we came back. We don't need that hassle."

His mind was busy figuring out the best way to make the hour trip back to his cabin. Taking the lowland route and skirting the lake seemed best.

Rita made an exasperated sound. "I think those Russian boys are more at home in the city than out here. I can't see them setting an ambush."

He shook his head and was glad it didn't make him dizzy. "That was the first bunch. I expect they've recruited different folks by now. There are a lot of forests in the Motherland. The worst thing we can do is underestimate the enemy."

She gave him a curious look. "You call them an enemy. Why? That has a lot of connotations that words like opponent wouldn't have."

"They called the shots on this one. As far as I'm concerned, the slate was clean after my little altercation with Tony. The Russian mob, with their particular set of values, took things to this level, and now we have several people dead. This is far from over."

It took them an hour and a half to get back to the cabin because they made their own trail, and some of it was rough going. Although he was feeling better, he had to stop a few times and catch his breath, fighting dizziness and nausea. When he stopped, Rita would stand next to him, holding him and saying how sorry she was.

"Dammit, stop apologizing..." His hand whipped out and stopped her from replying.

They stood on the shady side of a huge oak, and something ahead of them caught his attention. With a gentle hand, he pushed her down and looked around.

The wind caressed the tops of the trees around them, and he could hear the groaning timber—branches and small trees rubbing together. A cedar tree, upwind from them, gave up its fragrance to the windy day but didn't give up the sounds of the birds that would be feeding on the berries under its protective cloak of boughs. No birds. No squirrels barking. In the distance, he could hear a powerboat on the lake.

They were close to the cabin, and he knew Sally wouldn't come alone. He walked around the tree and spoke in a normal voice.

"Shepherd. We're coming in."

About fifty feet away, a figure rose in the fern and sumac, wearing a ghillie suit adorned with sticks and fronds from where he was hiding.

"How the hell did you know? Sally said you were good, but so am I. There's no way I gave myself away."

"Son," Jim gave the man a serious glance, "the first thing you need to learn is, no matter how good you think you are. there's always someone better or luckier." He glanced at an amazed-looking Rita holstering her pistol and then back at the camouflaged man. "Besides, I heard you snoring."

"My ass, you did. Now, get on down to the cabin. Sally's waiting. I got a nap to take here." With that, the man sunk back down into the fern.

Jim hoped the Shepherd would change position in case someone watched. The camaraderie of the Shepherds was a great thing, although few of them knew each other personally. For their own protection, they could pass each other on the street and not recognize the other.

Rita walked close enough their shoulders were touching. "How did you know?"

He shrugged. "It wasn't so much something I saw, but the realization that he had to be there. Just a gut feeling, I guess."

The door to the cabin leaned against the wall, so they walked unannounced into the gloomy interior. The windows had black trash bags taped over them. They went through the house and onto the back deck.

A small, dark-complexioned woman dressed in jeans and a pull-over sweatshirt jumped from her chair and came over to hug Rita.

"Hi. I'm Sally. It's good to meet you. Thanks for bringing in the dumbass." She turned to Jim and eyed him critically. "You look like shit. And what's with this bombed-out-looking Sarajevo house? I've seen better looking places in Bosnia, or worse yet, Detroit."

Jim shook his head. "I had a little welcoming committee, sort of a neighborhood outreach. I haven't had time to clean up after the party." He still stood with his arms out, smiling. "No hug?"

Her reply was grumpy but a little forced. "I don't hug guys, period." She turned to Rita. "He knows that." Turning back to Jim, she continued. "And I don't hug operatives at all. You know that too. Besides, we have business to discuss."

He waited, wiggling his fingers in a 'come here' fashion. "Come here, you little minx."

In two steps, she was in his arms, crushing him in her embrace, her head tight against his chest. It looked like a storm cloud was brewing over Rita until he shook his head at her.

Sally stepped back from him but kept a grip on his arms. "Damn you, why didn't you let us know where you were? To just disappear...? You have friends who care. We looked for you, Jim. After that Mexican fiasco, you dropped off the face of the earth."

He tried to shrug free but couldn't break her grip on

his arms. "Maybe I didn't want to be found. After that last assignment, I walked away and was through with all that."

"Yeah, well, it's a good thing your lady found our number." Sally grinned at him. "Why was it there? Freudian slip? Were you thinking of calling us? Just handy because you missed me so much?"

It was Rita's turn to sound grumpy. "I hate to break up this little reunion, but I need to go to town. I hate it, but there are a couple of families I need to visit for a bereavement call."

He turned toward her. "I'll go..."

Sally interrupted forcefully. "No."

Both turned to stare at her.

She stepped away from Jim so she could address both. "Things have changed in two days. Our people in town don't have everything figured out yet, but we have most of it. I need to fill you in."

He stared at her a moment and then relaxed. "All right, Sally. Is this a full-on Shepherd response?"

"No. At least, not officially. Everything going on here is on the QT and it's all on personal time. We have a few assets gathering information."

"I thought your little Alaska puddle jumper only seated four?"

Sally snickered. "I had a couple sitting between the aisles. The pilot was pissed because of the weight, but he got over it. Like I said, you have friends."

He felt Rita's hand rubbing his back with a soft, feather touch. "He has friends here too."

He gave her a curious look before speaking to Sally. "So...?"

"Okay." Sally briskly rubbed her hands together.

"First is the City of White Rock. Viktor has been busy and his meddling may have helped us, not on purpose of course. I don't know how much money it took, but as of now, no shooting has occurred."

Rita looked at them with wonder and he could see anger flushing her face. "There were people there. Hell, half the sheriff's posse was there. People know."

"Sheriff's posse?" Sally shook her head and then continued. "The whole thing has been spun as a readiness exercise that went too far. The dispatcher has taken an extended vacation, as did the deputy. We think they cremated the bodies and then paid off the families."

"Impossible," Rita interjected. "Everyone—"

"—likes money." Sally's expression was grim.

He flinched away from the hand on his back that became a claw.

Sally shrugged. "The body of Fred Sazanov, a.k.a. Freddy the Shank, has disappeared. The county commissioners appointed Sanders interim sheriff. Rita, you resigned. They have an apparent signed document from you. The highway patrolman, Bob Detwiler, is assisting the new sheriff in his duties."

Rita still shook her head. "But—"

Sally waved her quiet. "Rita, concerning the double-nuts call you put out, as far as we can tell, the other counties are going with the emergency exercise gone too far. The responding counties are pissed, and a couple of the sheriffs want to talk to you in person and right away. I believe forthwith is the word they used—I thought that word was only used on TV. The rumor flying about is that all this may have led to your resigning." She did the double air-quote with her fingers at the word resigning.

"So, truth having left the building, things are quiet in

the old hometown—all tied up in a nice, neat package. The rumor mill is going, but that will go away soon. You gotta hand it to these guys. If nothing else, they are efficient."

"Well, isn't that just too convenient." Rita's voice was low and hoarse. "I still say it's impossible. There are families involved. People will figure it out."

Sally shrugged. "Oh, I'm not saying it won't all fall apart. It will, sooner or later. The Russians don't care about that. All they need are a few days for it to all hang together, and then they'll disappear, leaving the locals holding a bag of angry skunks."

"What about the rest of the Russian crew?" Jim asked.

"Oh, they're just hanging out. I think they're waiting for you to surface. That's why I don't want either of you to go to town. At least, don't go until we're ready. If they can't find either of you, we're okay."

"Won't they come back here to check?"

Sally shrugged. "They might, but if you move, they'll be sure to see you. The smart thing to do is wait a little longer. I shudder to think what would happen if you're in town and they decide to take you out. We don't need any kind of shootout, but one in town would be devastating." She gave Rita a hard look. "From what I've heard, half the town is armed and would love to join in. What is it with you people?"

Jim stood, feeling a heavy tiredness that threatened to consume him. He must have swayed a little because Rita jumped to his side, holding his arm.

"Ladies, since there's a guard outside, I'm going to my room and rest in a real bed for a while. We'll cool it for now, but I doubt it will last long. I have a feeling the

Russians won't give up." He met the gaze of each of them. "And I'm damned sure they know where we are, and I can't figure what they're waiting on."

Walking into his bedroom, he sat on the edge of his bed. Glancing at his bookcase, a quote came to mind. What was it Louie said? "You can't stop a man who's right and just keeps on coming." Well, he'd have to start that march another day. He fell backward on the bed, watching a spider make its way across the ceiling.

Another day...

———

THE TWO WOMEN stared at each other after Jim left. Rita broke the silence. "You seem to have a history with Jim. Anything I need to worry about?"

Sally laughed. "Well, that's direct and to the point. I could tell you it's none of your business just to yank your chain, but I won't."

She paused a moment and seemed to be gathering her thoughts. She sighed and pointed to her face. A thin scar ran from above her left eye down to her cheek.

"I used to be a field operative. I got careless and some very bad people captured me. Our firm knew my location and guessed that I was in trouble because I missed my check-in time along with a couple of other things. Given the situation and not wanting to ruffle political feathers, they decided I was dead or would be soon. So, the people in charge were sitting on their asses trying to formulate a plan to duck and cover so no fallout would land on them. I'm sure their plan included doing nothing.

"Jim was in the area, doing God knows what, and heard about it. He didn't need a plan, and he'd much rather ask for forgiveness than permission. How he found me, I'll never know. That magnificent man walked into that old warehouse where they held me, with guns blazing, and rescued me—took me right out of there while the brass was still pontificating."

She looked at Rita with tears in her eyes. "They'd already raped me several times and were going to behead me—the guy there had his sword and everything. Hell, by then, I didn't care. I just wanted it to end, one way or the other. You ever wonder why on the recordings they show on the internet, when they parade all the people out for the mass beheadings, that they're so docile looking? By that point, they welcome death."

She took a deep breath and continued while Rita stared, mesmerized by the story. "They had my head down, and the guy was just starting his swing when the shots rang out. I jerked back and got this little scar and lost my eye. I don't know how many men Jim killed to get to me, and don't care one bit. The last person between Jim and me was the man with the sword. It was like the scene from that old Harrison Ford movie, and at any other time, it would have been funny."

"The bastard charged Jim, screaming at the top of his lungs. Jim's Glock was empty, so he just pulled the little .357 Rossi out of his pocket—I'm betting he still carries it —and shot him. That thing packs a punch. After that, he wrapped my face to stop the bleeding, picked me up, and carried me out of there."

She grinned at Rita. "The rest is mundane history. I got a desk job and became Jim's friend, whether he wanted me or not. As I rose in ranks, I also vowed never to turn my back on anyone in the field. That's why it hurt so much when Jim disappeared."

"So, you're just friends?" Rita pressed for an answer.

"Yeah, sort of. That little experience kind of turned me off from romance. The shrinks said my distaste for a romantic relationship would fade with time, but to be honest, I'm not trying too hard. As for Jim, I don't know of anyone getting close enough to be friends with him. He's a loner. Maybe you'll make it with him, maybe not."

She sighed and held her gaze on Rita. "One thing you should know. If you hurt him, I'll kill you."

Rita snorted while pulling her hand over her face. "Well, you're one woman too late on that score. Seems a Russian girl got there first." Rita gave the woman a quick rundown on that situation—the start of it all. "If you don't mind, I'd rather be your friend. And if I ever hurt him—well, hurt him again. It sure as hell won't be intentional."

She backed away from Sally a moment, holding up her hands. "Wait. Does a concussion count?"

The other woman laughed. "Oh, hell no. I've wanted to do that to him for a long time."

The sound of tires on gravel and a vehicle approaching interrupted them.

TWENTY-THREE

A CAR DOOR slamming outside brought Jim out of a restless sleep. He found himself sitting upright on the edge of the bed. His heart pounded and he was confused a moment. Russians? The voices in the front room sounded friendly enough. His feet were still on the floor. It felt like his backup pistol left a permanent imprint in the small of his back. He figured he'd sat down and passed out—a bad habit if you wake up groggy. Curious, he got up and walked into the other room.

The women were talking to a tall man wearing an open-collared checkered shirt tucked into jeans. The boots the man wore looked scuffed on the front. He had law enforcement stamped all over him, and he followed Jim's entry into the room with cold, gray eyes. Jim started a casual reach for a weapon.

Sally interceded. "Relax, Jim. This is Lieutenant Barnes. He's in charge of the highway patrol that covers this area. I called him last night and briefed him on the problem. At least what I know of it."

The man extended his hand to Jim. "Nice to meet you, Mr. Lane. Thanks for not shooting me."

Jim had to smile at the humor as he shook hands with the man. "Sorry about that. There's been a lot going on."

Rita interrupted. "I've put together some sandwiches if anyone is interested. Jim, you need to seriously stock your fridge." They all headed for the kitchen table. "Lieutenant, what would you like to drink?"

He pointed at the refrigerator. "Does that still work with the bullet holes in it?"

"Good enough," Rita said. "It's leaking a little air."

Barnes snorted. "Beer, if you have it. And call me Josh. I'm not on duty. At least, not now." He looked around at them. "And it's a damned good thing. This whole situation has gone to shit if you'll pardon my French."

Jim spoke around his ham sandwich. "I'm sitting here with a half-pint operative from an unnamed organization, a defrocked county sheriff, an off-duty highway patrolman, someone hiding outside in a ghillie suit who I hope to hell is my friend, and a small army of Russian mob floating around waiting for me to make a move. What could possibly go wrong in this situation?"

"By the way." Barnes pointed at Jim's shotgun. "Is that legal? I've seen a lot of hardware, but only half the stuff you have on it. An autoloader drum on a shotgun? Gimme a break."

Jim looked at the AA12 leaning against the wall. "It's all over-the-counter stuff. We have a lot of quail and dove around here. I'm a bad shot, so I need lots of chances."

"Really?"

"I kid you not."

Barnes did an eye roll, and they all gave attention to their sandwiches. After a few moments, he broke the silence again.

"Like I said, the situation has changed from last night when Sally called. I guess the mortician got drunk and talked." He glanced at Rita. "Just so you know, most of the law enforcement in other counties know you personally and never believed for one moment that you'd transmit a double-nuts call as a training exercise. You'd be amazed at how many cars are hanging around your county line. They know something is wrong. You have friends, Rita."

Rita's voice was gruff. "Well, I'd hope they knew better."

"So now, the new adjusted storyline coming out of White Rock is that Mr. Lane went to the sheriff's office to finish the job on the man who attacked him. While doing that, he killed the dispatcher and the deputy. To back that up, they have some .40 cal shell casings found at the scene." He glanced at Jim, but both were startled by a gasp from Rita.

She had her hand to her mouth, her eyes wide. "I told Detwiler that Jim didn't kill them because he carries a Glock 22. That's a forty caliber just like mine. I'm betting that's where they came up with the right shell casings for evidence. And I didn't see any shell casings when I did my walk-through. I'm so sorry. I shouldn't have run my mouth."

The patrolman was examining his beer label. "Jim, should I assume that's not the only pistol you carry?"

He gave the man an uneasy glance, knowing where the next questions were going. "I carry a snub-nosed Rossi .357 revolver."

Barnes nodded. "Nice piece. Ammo?"

"Hollow points. It's for close work." Jim gave the patrolman a puzzled look.

"Hell, if the frags don't kill them, the noise will." His gaze locked on Jim. "I don't suppose you can prove you didn't do any of these shootings?"

Jim looked at the man for a moment. "Nope. I came here that night after I woke up from being knocked on the head."

He looked pointedly at a blushing Rita. "And then I vacated right before the assault on my house. I even watched them do it. There were three vehicles, but I didn't get a head count of personnel. You'll notice my new decor. I'm thinking of submitting it to HGTV. I'll call it Early American-*Last Stand at Papago Wells*."

Barnes finished his sandwich and washed it down with beer. "No, that doesn't work. I read that book. That was all rocks. And desert. There's something that works better, but I just can't bring it up right now."

He seemed to be thinking about something. "I always judge people by what they do, not what they say. You can also judge a man by his weapons and friends. I saw your gun safe, got one about like it myself. But what do you have under that window valance by the front door?"

"I thought that was hidden pretty good. Hell, the Mafia goons didn't find it." Jim went to the front door and brought back a rifle. "It's a Henry Big Boy. It fires a .44 mag."

Barnes took it and looked it over, confirming it was loaded. "Do you have the matching pistol?"

"Of course. It's a Virginia Dragoon with *We the People* inscribed on the butt plate."

"Sweet." The patrolman looked askance at him. "Are you a sugar gun, faster than the blink of an eye?"

Jim laughed. "Nobody pulls a .44 mag in a hurry. It's too heavy and it bucks like a mother. Why?"

"I used to do some cowboy-mounted shooting contests, you know, where they ride a pattern shooting at balloons? Lots of fun."

"I've seen those. There'd be too much recoil with this load."

Barnes handed the rifle back. "Still, they are sweet shooters. When we get this mess cleaned up, I'd like to come out and shoot with you. I'll bring the beer." He grinned. "We'll drink it after the shooting, of course."

He paused a moment and his expression turned serious. "I need to talk to Sally and then go check in. After that, I may have to come back officially. Look, about that future visit. I owe her, and I believe the sheriff's word, so you've got some good people in your corner. However, it might hamper the immediate investigation if you were here. If you see me coming, go fishing or something. You get my drift?"

"Wait a minute." Rita retrieved her phone from her shirt pocket. "I just remembered something, Lieutenant Barnes. It should help." The man winced at her using his official title.

"I took a video of the scene." She handed him her phone. "The battery is dead because I forgot to turn it off. I think you'll find it very enlightening. For the record, I think the murder weapon was a .22 autoloader with a suppressor attached. Very professional. Something an enforcer for the mob would use."

Barnes shrugged. "You can buy that on any street corner."

She was shaking her head. "Not with a suppressor. Those are special ordered and very hard to get. There would be a record." She paused in thought. "Unless it was homemade."

He contemplated that a moment and then nodded his head. "Point taken. Of course, we're dealing with some folks who have access to all those things. We need a cord and computer."

Jim looked at the charging port on the phone. "I have it. Same as last time. And for the record, her phone is never charged. Let's get this movie fired up."

It took them a few minutes to get the video downloaded to Jim's computer. After viewing the video, they were each lost in thought. They didn't look at each other. Both women were blinking back unshed tears while Barnes softly cursed to himself.

Jim saved the movie to a USB memory stick, handed it to the patrolman and raised his eyebrows.

Taking the hint, Barnes stood up. Clearing his throat, his voice was still harsh. "Oddly enough, none of the on-scene investigators managed to take any pictures."

He paused a moment. "Okay. Here's the unofficial version of what's going down—at least my intent. Patrolman Detwiler will get a summons to present himself forthwith to HQ in Springfield. He won't be back. If he runs, we'll find him. Since this involves a county sheriff, and at your request, State will take over the situation and investigate. Rita, don't be surprised to see your signature on request forms. At the end of all this, I expect to see you reinstated as the sheriff. Once things quiet down, you can resign as you wish. If that happens, we'll initiate a special election for the position and for all the county commissioners. The current commissioners are gone, regardless.

"Every rabbit trail of money that's been spread around by the Russians will be followed and prosecuted in one way or another. With possible foreign nationals involved, I'm tempted to call in Homeland Security. However, I don't think anyone could stand the media frenzy involved with that."

He paused to take a drink from the fresh bottle of beer that Rita slid across the table. "All this will take some time, and I'm hoping to keep it very quiet. If the fourth estate does get hold of this, we'll be up to our eyeballs in reporters. That means you, Jim. I don't want you going to town and getting into some big gunfight with Viktor and his people. I know you have cause, but let us handle them."

Jim nodded with a grim smile. "What if they come to me?"

"I'm aware of your capabilities. I'm also aware of what Shepherds can do." The man's expression was cold as he held Jim's gaze. "Look, I understand what you're doing and why. I commend it. It puts you in a lot more danger but keeps things out of town and semi-isolated. Those boys are all over White Rock trying to make sure they have the advantage in town. That's where they want all this to go down. If you drive into town, they'll box you in and your truck will look like swiss cheese from all the bullet holes. But they are not in their element out here."

He finished his beer. "That being said, you have every right to defend yourself. Just keep the civilian population out of it. We both know if word of this gets out, the local spit-whittle-and-chew club will grab their guns and go after anyone they think resembles a Russian. God knows who that would be, probably everyone with a crew cut. The Baldknobbers are only a few generations away from us. We don't need that kind of grief."

He looked back at them on his way out. "Sally has my number. If anything comes up that I need to know, have her contact me." Cold eyes surveyed them for a moment. "I'm going way out on a limb here. Things will happen. I'd better not find out y'all have lied to me. About anything."

He went a few steps toward a charcoal-colored Dodge Charger that anyone over four years old would recognize for a cop car, then stopped and spoke to Jim.

"I've got it. *Last of the Breed.* You're not Native American, are you?"

Jim shook his head. "Nope. English back to the fourteenth century."

"The Battle of Agincourt? Maybe a Welsh bowman?"

He nodded. "A bad day for the French."

They watched him drive away in silence.

Sally spoke up. "Wow. That man takes charge in a hurry. Anyway, I need to take some lunch to the outpost."

"About that guard, he needs to move around some and tell him to keep an eye on his six, not just the road. We about walked right over him coming in."

"I'll tell him. He's new and needs experience. Rita, can you help me with the food? Jim, you need to do some repairs. For now, I think the black plastic over the windows is a good idea. No one can see in. But we need to put the front door back in place. Somehow, it makes me feel safer."

"Aye, Captain." He saluted and headed for the utility room and his tools before she bounced something off his head.

He sidetracked to his gun safe. He'd purchased a used Canon Scout at a garage sale of all places, and could see new scuff marks on the door where someone tried to pry it open. The thing weighed close to eight hundred pounds, so he wasn't surprised they didn't breach the door. He'd reinforced the floor just to hold it.

Keying in the combination, he turned the spoked wheel to open the door. "You need to arm yourselves better. Never can tell when visitors will come again."

Rita helped him hang the outside door. The battery on his screw gun went dead, so they wound up using nails. If they had time later, he'd fix it. If not, it wouldn't matter.

When he tried to get a tactical vest on Rita, she objected. "I've got all that stuff in my Jeep. I'll go get it."

"I wouldn't." Sally came breezing through the door. "I have someone coming in the morning to check your vehicles for IEDs. Until then, don't touch anything."

She saw the look on their faces and nodded. "You didn't think of that, did you?" she continued after a moment. "When that happens, I'll be sending the sentry back. The way things are going, I don't think we'll need him."

Jim spoke to Sally. "Would you consider leaving now? And take Rita with you? My gut feeling is that it's going to get ugly around here."

Sally paused a moment and then nodded. "You may be right. I think we've done all we can with the situation in town. I don't know how much more help we can be. I'll think about it. We've got some time before dark."

He looked outside. "We've wasted most of the day. I'll rest some more and then plan on scouting the area tonight. Anything happens out of the ordinary, wake me."

TWENTY-FOUR

JIM'S EYES SNAPPED OPEN. Something was wrong. Before he was fully awake, he swung his feet off the bed and onto the floor, pausing for a moment to get his bearings. The south window was open, and a breeze ruffled the curtain. He kept it open because it was a sheer drop of about twenty feet to the ground, so he didn't worry about someone sneaking through.

His fingers ran through his hair. At least he didn't have a headache. He listened for a moment and heard the sound that tripped his subconscious alarm bell. Someone was running on the gravel drive.

He grabbed his two pistols from the nightstand, slung the shotgun over his shoulder, and crept into the living room. When the front door burst open, he almost shot her.

"Jesus, Rita. What's going on?" Keeping the door open, he looked outside long enough to see a man in camo move off the lane and into the trees.

He spoke again, watching the front. "What happened?"

She tried to straighten, looking like a sprinter with a cramp, her hand holding her side and trying to catch her breath. "Sally didn't come back. You were sleeping, and I didn't want to wake you. I went to check on her."

"You didn't know where to look, did you?"

"No. I swear I need to get out of this business. I just went up the lane and called out." She paused a moment. "Two men came out of the brush carrying what looked like M-4s. I didn't know whose side they were on, so I started running. I can't believe it. I'm armed and I ran. I guess they didn't want me."

"Oh, I'm sure they want you, just all in one piece." Jim began checking the shotgun, making sure the magazine was full. He racked a shell into the chamber and then fed another into the magazine.

Hesitating a moment, he left the sling attached to the shotgun. "You did the smart thing. Don't ever fight a battle on their terms. An old general once said getting into a fair fight just shows a lack of preparation on your part."

"Since they haven't attacked the cabin, there may just be a few of them out there—probably to keep us bottled up until the troops arrive." He started out the back way, walking with a cold knot of fear in his belly for Sally. "Watch the front. Cover me if you can. I've got a feeling there are no friendlies out there."

"Let me catch my breath. I'll go with you."

He spoke over his shoulder. "No way. You need to guard the castle in case we come back with company."

She yelled at him to stop and rushed to him. Grabbing the front of his vest, she pulled him in for a kiss. "Please be careful. You have a wild look in your eyes and I don't like seeing you out of control."

Out of control. Fitting. "This is the part of me I'd hoped you'd never see." His gaze was on the open door. "They won't like it either."

"What are you going to do?"

It was a good question. If he thought too much about it—he probably wouldn't do it. It would all depend on surprise. Only a crazy person would do what he was going to do. The men he was going against may be ex-soldiers or mercenaries, but he'd bet their experience was in cities and the sandbox. It was a crap shoot any way he looked at it.

"I'm going up that hill after Sally. I can't leave her with them."

Her shoulders slumped. "I know. You must love her a lot."

He tipped her chin up with his finger. "I do...but not like that. You understand?"

She nodded, tears in her eyes. "I guess. Be careful."

He grinned at her. "Careful won't work. Not today." A good bet was that going down the back stairs would get him shot. Stopping in front of the sliding glass patio doors, he moved a heavy rug to reveal a trapdoor. Pulling up the door by the recessed ring, he smiled at her.

"Bolt hole. Every castle has one. Put the rug back when I'm gone and then watch the front."

His emergency escape route brought him out below the back deck and into complete cover. He paused a moment and then skirted around the bottom of the house. It didn't take long to find the man they'd left to watch the side stairs leading to the deck. The man crouched behind a fallen tree about a hundred feet away, rising occasionally to look around.

Every time the man lowered his head, Jim would

advance. He was standing behind the sentry within five minutes. As the man popped up again, Jim glided behind him, grabbed him by the hair, and cut his throat. Almost in the same motion, he shoved him forward over the fallen tree trunk and stepped back into the trees. It was brutal and fast, but he knew the Russians would offer no quarter to any of them. With Sally in danger, he didn't have time to fool around.

The Shepherd sentry's last position was straight up the hill from him. He'd bet a pile of money the man never moved the entire time he was there. He hoped it didn't prove to be a fatal rookie mistake.

The sound of a shot came from the house and the round ricocheted off something up the hill. He realized Rita was trying to get their attention and give him a little cover. Holding his shotgun at a ready position, he went charging through the thick brush, dodging and weaving through the undergrowth, around clumps of deadfalls and stumps. The noise cover earned him a few precious steps.

A man in camouflage gear stepped out from behind a tree and snapped off a shot at him. Jim's return fire tore a chunk of bark from the tree and took most of the man's arm with it. As he fell to the ground screaming, another shot punched him in the chest.

Jim paused long enough to feed shells into the magazine and catch his breath. His head hurt and he felt weak, but ignored it. He tossed the man's guns into the brush before continuing up the hill. There was no use leaving extra firepower lying around for the enemy to use.

The shotgun blasts and screaming took away all thoughts of stealth. Using what cover he could, he advanced toward the crest. He knew they could hear him but doubted they had a visual.

At a flicker of movement ahead, he dropped to the ground. In near silence, he moved to his left and then came up behind their position. Since he was on the uphill side, he could see into the little clearing they occupied. The Shepherd in the ghillie suit lay sprawled out and partly covered Sally. He could see a large red stain in the middle of the man's back. Scratch one, Shepherd.

Two men crouched close by, looking down the hill. They had suppressed M-4s, so that's why he didn't hear shooting. One of Sally's bare legs moved. It may have been reflex, but he was going in. If she was still alive, there wasn't much time.

Dropping down into the clearing, and with no thought of rules or protocol, he pumped four shots into them and the twelve-gauge zombie loads didn't leave much for their kinfolk to mourn.

Slinging the shotgun over his back, he turned and rolled the man off her. She was alive, and he saw wounds on her side and shoulder. A lot of blood loss, but maybe not fatal. Maybe. There wasn't time to check her over better. He picked her up, draped her over his shoulder and away from the hot barrel of the shotgun, and started toward the cabin.

As he walked toward the road, a man dressed in black stepped out from behind a tree with his rifle pointed at Jim's belly. He felt a cold chill, cursing himself for being lax. Concern for Sally had overridden caution.

The man glanced behind Jim at the bodies and then shrugged. "You might as well put her down. You're not going anywhere."

Jim stopped moving, realizing they were alive

because the man was a talker. "Are you the last of them? I took care of the other four."

"Yeah." The man chuckled. "They weren't worth much, but they were cheap. I guess you get what you pay for."

"So, what do you get paid?" Jim stalled, trying to come up with something. Any kind of distraction. The barrel of the rifle pointed at his belt buckle and didn't waver. Neither did the man's gaze.

"Oh, I get paid really good. But that makes no difference to you. I'm going to enjoy killing you. Viktor said we'd get a bonus if we kept you alive, but I don't think that's going to work out. Once you're out of the way, I'll get the woman at the house." The man gave a leering grin, and the barrel of his rifle wavered and went off center. "That's the real prize. She's a fine piece. It was too bad she ran off before I could wound her. Viktor will have to be satisfied with seconds."

Jim shook his head, speaking in a calm tone. "Viktor is a dead man. For that matter, so are you."

His pistol was in a belly holster and the talker couldn't see it because of Sally. When Jim shifted her weight on his shoulder, the man's gaze followed the movement for a second. It was enough. The rubberized grip came naturally into his sweaty hand. The man's eyes widened as he tried to bring his rifle in line. Jim shot him twice in the belly. His third shot ricocheted off the rifle and tore a bloody furrow into the man's chest. The talker was dead before he hit the ground—dead of another axiom. Never talk when it's a shooting matter.

"You were overpaid, sport." He shifted her weight again and the movement brought a moan from Sally as he headed toward the cabin. Although she didn't weigh more than a hundred pounds, he was panting in a cold sweat by the time he got there.

Rita met him at the door with a worried look and reached out to help. Once they laid Sally down, she came up with her phone and started punching numbers.

He put his hand out to her. "Don't call 9-1-1. That'll just bring out the new acting sheriff and the rest of Kumarin's little army."

"She needs help now and we can't use the Jeep or your truck. We have to do something."

Grabbing a small med kit from a kitchen cabinet, Jim pulled out a roll of gauze fill with a quick clotting agent. Pulling his knife, he cut off a two-foot piece and stuffed it into the exit wound. He rolled Sally onto her back; her weight would keep pressure on that part of the wound. Another piece of gauze went into the entry wound.

During this, Rita hadn't ceased her nervous chatter. Grabbing her hand, he had her put pressure on the wound. The amount of blood lessened within a couple of minutes. He didn't know if that was good, or if she was running out. The blood flow was never spurting, so there was a good chance an artery wasn't hit with the bullet. That gave her a chance.

His breath was returning to normal, and he vowed to himself to exercise more—if he lived. "Do you have a private number for any of the medics?"

"No, but I've got Dave's home phone number. His wife will have his cell number."

"All right. Make the calls and get him out here on the quiet. If you can find Sally's cell phone, see if Barnes is on the contact list. If he is, call him and tell him every-thing you know. Maybe that'll speed up his timetable."

"And, Rita..."

She looked up at his change of tone.

"When these idiots don't check in, Viktor will be coming. He has to be getting low on personnel, so he'll have to come himself."

He took a deep breath. "You go out with the ambulance. If you won't take it as an order, then do it as a favor to me. I'm asking. You go. I can't deal with this if I'm worrying about you. Just figure you're protecting Sally and the ambulance crew."

"I want to stay and help. My shooting is just as good as those mercenaries. Let me stay and watch your back."

His hand gently squeezed her shoulder, gaze settling on her dark-blue eyes. "You're not mean enough, Rita. I'm sorry, but you're not. Besides, as the future reinstated sheriff of Limestone County, you don't want to see what I'm going to do."

He paused a moment. "And shouldn't see what I've already done. You go with the EMS crew."

Her voice was soft as she dug out Sally's phone. "All right."

He turned and pulled out his own phone and punched in a number he knew from memory—one he never expected to call again.

"This is Shepherd Lane. Yes, that one. Dammit, stop talking and start recording. Listen to me. You have one Shepherd killed. I don't know his name. Sally is wounded. She'll go to Mercy Hospital in Springfield, Missouri. Coordinate her care from your end and provide security."

Jim listened a moment and then interrupted. "No. Do not respond with assets. I'll handle this." When the voice on the other end of the call started talking again, he listened for a moment and then interrupted.

"Look, I know what the protocol is and that you want to help, but I'll handle the cleanup. This is personal." Again, he listened and then sighed. "No. Any damage control needs to go through Lieutenant Josh Barnes, Troop D, Missouri Highway Patrol."

He glanced at Rita before continuing. "We have enough people hurt because of me. There will be no other assistance required." He hung up with the other party still talking.

Rita still kneeled beside Sally, watching him with her mouth open. Tears started to escape her eyes. Her expression looked as if she'd just seen her first UFO. "Who did you...? What the hell are you going to do, Jim? No. Forget I said that. You need to go out with us."

"I'm going to do what I should have done in the first place. I should have killed that peckerwood the first time I saw him. It would have saved a lot of grief. Call your medic friend and get him out here. Have him transport Sally to the hospital. As soon as you're away, call Barnes and get him up to speed."

His smile was cold. "Once that is done, place that 9-1-1 call. I want them to know exactly where I am."

She started to respond but he turned away.

"Jim." She reached him in two steps and hugged him in a fierce grip. "Please don't do anything stupid."

He extricated himself from her knowing she felt shut out, but it had to be that way. Raising her chin, he kissed her. "I've been doing stupid things since this mess started. There's no reason to stop now."

Her breath was soft on his face. "So, was I one of your stupid things?"

"No. I think we've been at odds with each other. It's time to start pulling together."

TWENTY-FIVE

THINKING there might be an hour of lag time before things started popping, he went outside and ran to his shed to get the Gator four-wheeler and tow ropes. If there were explosives in the vehicles, he was sure the detonation would be electrical. Turn on the key, and boom. There wouldn't have been time for anything else. He was sure the vehicles were safe. Pretty sure.

Using a tire iron to break out the driver-side window, he reached in and shifted her Jeep to neutral. The tow ropes were fifty feet long, so he hooked two of them together, attached one end to the back bumper of Rita's Jeep, and started the four-wheeler forward. It was a heavy vehicle, and he spun out a lot of gravel, but it started to move.

Nothing. No explosion. He used the same method and pulled his pickup the same way. He left both vehicles at the beginning of the lane next to the highway. If someone pulled into the drive, like people driving large SUVs with tinted windows, he could disable it right there and make a bottleneck.

Now the house was clear of obstructions and he had a clear field of fire right up to the Jeep and pickup. The last thing he needed, if he decided to defend the house, was a carload of hostiles unloading right on his doorstep.

He went inside to find Rita sitting on the floor with Sally's head on her lap. It looked like the bleeding had stopped, but Sally was pale and her breathing was shallow. "Can you tell how she's doing?"

Rita shook her head. Blood from her hands made a streak on her cheek when she'd wiped away a tear. "I can't wake her up. The medics are on the way and should be here soon. I told them to keep it quiet until we tell them different."

She looked up at him with a grimace. "It's a damned good thing there's still some loyalty floating around out there. He didn't question anything."

"You're that kind of person, Rita. You should know that." He kneeled by them a moment with a silent prayer and then stood watch by the front door, looking for any movement between them and the road. Five men were down, and he needed to do something about their bodies. The body count was rising in this whole mess and it left a cold knot in his stomach.

He was certain that count was going to rise. Viktor would be coming with the next load of mercenaries and that would be a whole new ball game. All he had to do was keep from being part of that count.

The big modular ambulance pulled into the drive, snapping his mind back into focus. They swung around and backed up to the porch, the backup alarm breaking the calm. As the two men exited and tried to take a gurney out the back doors, he stopped them.

"No time."

Returning to Sally, he stooped and picked her up. With Rita right behind him, he stepped into the ambulance and lay her on the cot. He backed out, making room for the medics.

As the two-man crew worked to start a line for fluids, Rita came up behind him. "I thought about knocking you out again so we could take you with us. If I hadn't already softened up your head once, I'd have done it."

He reached out and brought her trembling body to him. Her expression was soft and pleading before she leaned her head against his chest. This was something he'd not seen from her. She was always the alpha female.

"It has to be this way, Rita."

"Why?" Anger made her voice hoarse. "Once I call Barnes, this place will be swarming with highway patrol and deputies from other counties. Let them do their job."

"Their job? That's the problem. Those men and women will do their job, or try. And, you know what kind of man Viktor is. Do you think he'll give up without a fight? I don't think so. They have a different mindset. While a police officer is wondering if they should shoot, these clowns will already be shooting. You should know that by the way you lost your husband. Your way will get some more good people killed. Those officers have families and need to go home to them. They don't need to die out here—not for this—not for something I caused. These wannabe bad boys from the mob have killed too many good people already. Don't you see, Rita? This is my fault. All of it. It started with Alina and Tony. Now, I need to end it."

"So that's it? You're going to pull all the killers to you just to keep people out of harm's way?" She grabbed him by the arm and pulled him toward her. "You have family too. There's Sally and me. And your way will get you killed. Is that what you want? Is it? You looking to check out in a blaze of glory?"

He shook his head and snorted before looking away toward the forest watching for movement. "Imagine pulling your finger out of a pool of water. I'll leave no more impression on this world than that."

Alpha female came back. "Oh come off it. That's a lie and you know it. Is that part of your machismo? No one cares for poor little me?" She squeezed his arm harder. "People care. Sally cares. I care. Don't pull that shit with me."

He stared into her eyes a moment while his thumb caressed around her lips. Her anger peaked, and he watched her try to control it.

His response was deliberately mild. "You're going to bruise my arm."

"It's usually the other way around." She laid her forehead on his chest again. "I have a history of leaving bruises on you."

He held her tight for a moment. "I want you to know I'll do my best to let you continue that."

The medics were motioning for her to get on board, and she turned to go. "Promise me? No matter what it takes? You stay alive. I don't care how mean and dirty you get or what you do. Stay alive for me."

He nodded and watched her climb into the back with Sally. As they pulled away, he could see her punching numbers into her cell.

The breeze came strong off the lake as the wind picked up. A gust came down the lane, making a small dust devil before dissipating when it hit the house. He lowered his head and closed his eyes until the dust and grit settled, wishing he could keep doing that—just close his eyes until it all went away.

———

THE AMBULANCE BEARING Sally and Rita hadn't been gone fifteen minutes when he heard a vehicle coming. So much for an hour lag time. He stood just inside the front door and watched one SUV pull in and stop. Maybe they were running out of troops.

For a moment, Jim thought again of the body count. Dead bodies were piling up like a Chicago weekend. Three were innocents. The rest he didn't care about. So far, he'd been running on a little skill and a lot of luck, and luck was a fickle mistress. She's a real bitch if pushed too hard.

The more he thought of it, he knew this place was untenable. This was his home, and he wanted to defend it. If he abandoned it, maybe it would still be standing if he returned. *If* was the operative word. All his reasons for drawing the Russians' attention were sound. Just not in this place. He needed to be mobile.

He reached inside and brought out the lever action rifle he'd shown Barnes. Three shots sounding like cannon fire sent lead through the radiator and ricocheted off the engine. Two more rounds went for the front tires. That should be an attention-getter.

The doors to the SUV opened and four men dove into the brush. One turned and began firing with his M-4. Jim watched the dust trail of bullets fall short of the house and then march up the lane toward him as the shooter adjusted.

Jim stepped back inside and moved to a window.

Ripping away the black plastic, he emptied the magazine into the weeds on both sides of their vehicle. Amid the sounds of ricochets and yelling, no one returned fire. He put his prized Big Boy inside the gun safe, closed the door, and spun the wheel.

He took a moment to look at the shambles of his house. It looked like a major rehab job was in store for someone. Bullet holes pockmarked the walls. The floor had burn marks and bloodstains. He had no illusions about coming back to fix the damage. Lifting the trap-door, he was soon outside. Two minutes later, he was on the same trail he'd used two days before. On the way around the house, he'd grabbed the gun dropped by the first man he'd killed who was supposed to be watching the back of the cabin. Just a few steps down the trail, he stopped and emptied its magazine toward the SUV and surrounding brush and trees. One three-round burst returned toward him but went high. He threw the empty gun into the foliage.

Now, they'd follow.

TWENTY-SIX

THE MEN CHASING him had been at it an hour and made plenty of noise. He heard them find three of the men he'd killed earlier—heard them shouting back and forth in anger. He wondered why they were being so noisy.

His concussion-addled brain must have made him stupid. He'd already mentioned to Rita that the men who followed the last attack would be a different quality than those who came before. And they were herding him like a dumb sheep.

Herding?

He dove off the trail as searing pain tore through his hip. Rolling down a hill and into a gully, he felt and heard bullets pounding into the forest floor around him. The heavy thump of the rounds into the dirt told him this was a heavy caliber rifle. He kept moving—rolling and jumping, desperate to find cover.

Bruised and bleeding from a dozen cuts and a bullet wound, he found himself behind a lichen-covered limestone outcropping. He looked around and saw there was no easy way to get to him, and no easy way out. It would be dark in an hour since he was on the shady side of the hill.

About fifty feet up the hill lay his shotgun. The shooter must have read his mind, because two well-placed shots made the gun useless. Hitting that gun as it lay on the downslope was good shooting. It made him think they wanted him to move.

He still had his pistol and a knife. The little Rossi revolver was gone, covered in leaves and sticks somewhere up the hill.

Well, hell.

He pulled his pistol and checked the magazine. One thing about a Glock. It wasn't fancy, but it would shoot whether dirty or clean.

Viktor's voice carried down the hill. "Lane. This is a poor end for a man of your talents. A poor end."

Jim looked around the side of the hill. There wasn't much to give hope for a quick getaway. Old dead falls littered the hillside. Vines and scrub brush grew in the meager sunshine filtering through the trees. The face of the hill was dotted with limestone outcroppings like the one he used.

"It's not ended, yet. Why don't you come and get me?"

"We will, trust me. It'll be dark soon. I know you're hit, so we'll let you bleed awhile. When you went tumbling down the hill, we didn't see any night-vision gear with you. In fact, you don't have much equipment at all. We'll have you surrounded in no time."

The man laughed. "I've told the men to use knives since you won't be able to see them."

At the sound of Viktor's laughter, he wanted to shoot up the hill, but knew the pistol wouldn't have the range.

He wondered if Viktor could see where he was hiding. If he couldn't, that was an advantage.

The wound on his hip was more painful than dangerous. The bullet cut a jagged swath around his hip as he was turning, missing the hip bone. He was lucky his pack was still with him. He pulled a battle dressing from it, loosened his belt, and put the bandage on the wound. Tightening his belt made an effective pressure bandage.

Why did so many antagonists like to talk? There should be a two-word course in being a tough guy—shut up. Old Louie had it right. By talking, the man gave away more than he intended. He also provided a reason for Jim to move. His men hadn't surrounded him—yet. If he told his men to use knives, it was because they didn't want to be caught in their own crossfire in the dark.

Still under cover, he took a few steps toward the lake and saw a small trail going around the bottom of the bluff. It wasn't much more than a rabbit track. If he hadn't seen it from a few feet away, Viktor sure wouldn't see it from on top of the hill. If he went on hands and knees, it would give him cover. To stay in this place was to die.

He crawled around rocks and under fallen trees. Careful to make as little sound as possible, he made a slow ascent up the hill. A few minutes later, he was standing behind a tree, surrounded by waist-high fern and well above the position where he thought Viktor and his men were.

As he looked around, an idea came to him. It was nearing dark and they were close to the ravine and cul-de-sac where Old Red liked to bed down. It was a dangerous place because there was only one way out, at least for the feral hogs.

Seeing a slight movement below, he fired a couple of rounds down the hill and started running for the ravine.

Someone yelled, "There he is." He heard Viktor's voice screaming, "Get him!"

They fired at him as he entered the bedding ground and he knew that would drive the hogs farther into the little canyon. Turning to look, he saw three men following close behind, leaping over dead falls and clumps of brush. The Russians kept shooting and he hoped they'd run out of ammo and not stop to aim.

He could hear the pigs squealing nervously ahead as his legs drove him forward through the brush. His lungs felt on fire and he labored to breathe as he burst into them. Old Red's brood had grown, and he estimated over fifty pigs of various sizes and color were milling around, frightened by the sound of the firing behind him. Half of the hogs were adult. There were too many piglets to count.

Jim went plowing right through the surprised swine, dodging the older boars as they tried to gore him when he went by. When he got through, he turned and fired into them—creasing a couple of the piglets so they'd start squealing. Nothing enrages a mother pig like a squealing piglet. The rounds panicked them and the pigs stampeded downhill right into the startled Russians.

Instead of running or jumping into a tree, the men stopped and fired into the hogs and found they were damned hard to kill. The smell of blood incensed them more. Surrounded by boars and sows weighing over four hundred pounds, a few up to nine hundred, they didn't last long. One man tripped and went down screaming, and then the other two weren't far behind.

Jim turned his head. The noise settled down and he

knew by the next morning there wouldn't be anything left to find but indigestible clothing and bones. Reloading his pistol, he settled the pack on his shoulders. He thought about going for one of the Russian's guns, but decided he didn't want to chance it. If he lived through this, he'd give Old Red a pass from now on.

Maybe.

When he climbed out of the little canyon, he was surprised to find several gashes on his legs from the hogs. Believing he'd dodged the tusks, and in his adrenaline-fueled rush, he hadn't felt the wounds. He was losing blood in small, steady drips. Weakness would follow. And infection. He hoped he'd live long enough to worry about infection.

Viktor was still out there, and Jim knew what he had to do. He tried to focus his mind on the problem. This had to end. He was exhausted from blood loss and adrenaline hangover. A thought came to him. A few hundred yards up the hill was the hole. His last gamble would be that the Russian would want to gloat.

TWENTY-SEVEN

TWILIGHT WAS GIVING way to darkness when Jim put together a small fire. He'd done all the preparations he could in the little time he had. His legs were on fire from the many wounds, and the gash in his hip made him wince with each step. He'd pulled a small broken tusk from one of the deeper gouges in his right leg. An immature boar must have left him that present. Pigs were quick and nimble, a trait that was unappreciated except by the farmers who raised them.

His energy level was near zero when he sat on a rock to make tea. He'd emptied a couple of water bottles into the pot to boil, waiting for the tea bags. The tea would provide some energy and he could use the bags as an astringent to clean his wounds, if he lived.

He'd moved the protecting cover off the hole. The flat rock was oblong. Pulling it toward him and turning it would allow the rock to tip if you sat on it. Covering the exposed part of the hole with his Mylar blanket, he pegged the edges down and scattered leaves and sticks over it. It was hard work moving the rock as blood leaked from his wounds. As a last visual, he smeared blood from his wounds over his chest and abdomen.

It wasn't a long wait. He heard a small rustle of leaves and Viktor stepped into the firelight with his rifle pointed at him. The rifle looked to be a twin of the one used by the sniper. His first gamble paid off. Viktor wanted to gloat.

Jim indicated the rifle with a nod. "Do you people buy those in quantity?"

Viktor didn't speak for a moment, looking around and wary of a trap. "Your pistol. Be careful how you take it out. Lay it down."

He shrugged and complied, watching the Russian as he relaxed. "So, what now? I'm all done in."

The man was antsy, checking everything around them. Finally, he said, "What are you brewing? Something for your last meal? That's a tradition for you Americans, isn't it? A last meal before execution?"

Ignoring him, Jim picked up a couple of tea bags, lifted the lid, and put them in the pot, trapping the strings with the edge of the lid. "Just making a little tea. I thought it would go well on a cool night. Don't you?"

The Russian stood watching him, clearly puzzled. He looked like a mountain cat, wary of a trap but still wanting to get to the bait. "This isn't like you to give up. I'm going to kill you. You must realize this?"

He shrugged. "Maybe. Life is a gamble. I think we can agree on that. We're two professionals. Perhaps some negotiation would be in order. There's no one here but us."

Viktor grinned, nodding at him. "Ah. I get it now. You wish to bargain for your life? I don't think so. That was a nasty thing you did to my men. I could hear them screaming. Swine?"

Jim nodded to him, trying not to think of the little canyon.

Still wary, the Russian's gaze flicked around the area. "We have them in Russia. Much larger than yours."

"Well, of course they are."

Viktor snorted. "Sarcasm just before you die? You're a brave and foolish man. Oh, you can kick your pistol a little farther away if you don't mind."

Jim stretched out one leg, moving the Glock beyond a quick reach. "I didn't get away clean, and that's the main reason I've stopped. I lost a lot of blood, Viktor. My hip wound is still bleeding." He tried to pull his leg back in, hissing in pain. "So, what's it going to be?"

Viktor gave him a smile, the firelight playing across his face. "The end is inevitable. For one man, you've done an incredible amount of damage." He shrugged. "My men weren't the best, but all I could get on short notice. Now that we're at an end, it's a matter of honor. I must continue."

Jim sighed and then shrugged, reaching for the teapot. Viktor stepped back, watching closely. "Oh, come on, Viktor. Hot water against your gun?"

He poured two cups and set them down next to the fire. "Your choice."

Viktor came closer, glancing around with a puzzled expression. "Drink from one."

Jim picked up a cup, blowing across the hot liquid and then drank. He was right, it was a comfort on a cool night.

The Russian walked to the fire, pulling a pistol from his belt holster and laying down the rifle. "I'm not a fool.

You know you're going to die. You might die from the wounds you already have, who knows. Since you're dead either way, you'd poison both cups."

He stopped and kicked over the extra cup of tea. "I've always been a step ahead of you. You just didn't know it. From the beginning, you never had a chance. Goodbye, Mr. Lane."

"Goodbye, Viktor."

The end was almost anticlimactic. When Viktor raised his pistol, Jim stomped on a green stick that had a rock under it as a fulcrum, with the other end in the fire. Being fresh cut and under the rock, it didn't burn. He then jumped to the side, grabbing for the Glock as he went. Pieces of burning wood and sparks flew into the air.

Bringing his gun up, the Russian took a quick step back, tripped on the flat rock, and sat down hard. The slick, moss-covered rock did the rest. When it tipped, Viktor went backward into the hole, firing as he went. One of the rounds caught Jim in the arm.

The forest was quiet after the loud gunfire. Jim rose from where he lay and examined his arm. The wound was superficial, just a groove cut through the skin. But added to his other wounds, it was going to be a problem.

"Shit, that hurts."

He walked over to his improvised trap. The tarp and debris were all gone. He picked up Viktor's rifle and dropped it into the hole. Now, the only sign of their conflict was the skid marks on the rock after he moved it back over the hole.

Looking at the remains of his fire, he started kicking dirt over the flames. After taking a quick drink and then emptying the rest over the remains of the fire, he stuffed the empty teapot back into his pack. Shouldering the pack, he sighed, looking around at the dark forest. The train wreck his life had turned into was over, at least for now. Rita was in Springfield taking care of Sally. He figured after losing their money source the other mercenaries would leave, and an hour of walking would get him home. Maybe an hour and a half if he followed the ridgeline and didn't trip much.

"Hell with it. I'm sleeping in a bed tonight."

———

RITA WAVED goodbye to the driver of the modular ambulance that dropped her off at Jim's cabin. It was near twilight and the house appeared ominous even though she'd left it not long ago.

She and the ambulance crew pushed away the new SUV blocking the driveway. The oil and water collected under the vehicle made her wonder if it could ever be driven again. Looking at the holes in front, she figured Jim used the rifle he'd shown the highway patrolman. There was some major damage to the front of the vehicle.

In the distance, she heard faint sounds of gunfire. Stepping out to the porch, she strained to hear more. When no more sound came, she paced the porch, unable to keep still.

Should she go to help Jim? How? Where? Her stomach knotted in fear, she went back inside and sat at the kitchen table. A feeling of déjà vu washed over her, but she wasn't going to wait this time. She began gathering her weapons and backpack.

The sound of tires on the gravel drive interrupted her thoughts. Not wanting to be caught in the house, she rushed toward the back but stopped when she saw the flash of blue and red reflected in a mirror.

She turned back to the front door and watched Barnes's Charger coming down the lane, followed by a patrol car with lights flashing. Another blocked the entrance of the drive.

What the hell?

She met him at the door, laden with her pack and armament.

"You won't need any of that shit." Barnes walked by her, taking her pack as he went.

Once again, they sat at the kitchen table, this time with bottles of Dr. Pepper. Rita just sat back and waited for it.

"You were going to take them all on? In the dark? By yourself?" He laughed. "I'm glad I stopped you. You've got more balls than sense."

He looked at her a moment. "In a manner of speaking, of course. No offense? Gotta stay PC, you know."

She kept her expression neutral as she watched him, unable to keep her knee from bouncing impatiently. There were places to go, things to do.

He sighed. "All right. Here's what has gone down since I left."

Taking a sip from his bottle, he continued. "We've been watching the Kumarin family for over a year. When all your troubles came out, we received a couple of tips and decided to scoop them up. Our folks in St. Louis picked up Anton Ivanov and several of his henchmen. They got a distinct feeling it wasn't a surprise. I'm sure their lawyers will bond them out, but with ankle bracelets on, I think that part of the threat is gone."

She shook her head. "He can still give orders."

"True. But our new GPS units on their ankles also have excellent microphones and transmitters on them. They work like a cell phone." He toasted her with her bottle. "Ain't technology grand?"

"What about the locals?"

"That one is kinda funny." He shook his head before continuing. "We rounded up two SUV loads of men filling their tanks at the local convenience store in Hunter, just a few miles from here. We had them surrounded before they could do anything. A couple tried to get away through the store, but there was a meeting of the local morning coffee drinkers club going inside— most of them vets. When the Russians started waving their guns around, they didn't last thirty seconds—shot to rag dolls. Gotta love country folk."

"What about Viktor?"

"We didn't find him."

She flinched, remembering the shots she heard earlier and then brought herself under control. "I have a good idea where he is. What about the locals in White Rock?"

Barnes got up to leave. "Thanks to your video, Detwiler and Sanders are in custody. We're still running down the payoffs and money trail, but the commissioners have resigned. Gonna be a lot of empty positions to vote on soon. Rita, I..."

She glanced up when he stopped speaking. Tony One-Ball was standing in the doorway with a mountain of a man behind him. Both were pointing machine pistols at them. The pistols weren't very accurate, more of a spray and pray, but didn't need to be accurate at this range.

Barnes held his hands away from his body. "I have men outside. I don't know who you are, but you won't get away with this."

Rita replied, "This is Tony One-Ball. I told you about him."

He pointed his pistol at Rita. "You shut your mouth."

With a smile that didn't reach his eyes, he continued. "Your men are taking a rest." Tony motioned to the man beside him. "Gregory, why don't you divest these officers of their weapons? Then you can zip-tie them."

Rita stood, torn between anger and despair. She started to move toward the back door, but Tony's gun followed her and she stopped.

When Gregory started toward Rita, Barnes tried to step in front of him. Gregory whirled and brought his gun down on Barnes's head. As the patrolman fell, Gregory dropped on him and tied his hands and feet. He then emptied the patrolman's pockets and took his weapons.

Rita leaned against the table, submitting as the giant searched her. His hands lingered over her breasts and were very thorough coming up her legs. Both her firearms were taken and tossed on the table.

"Nice guns," Gregory said, smirking at her.

Rita ignored him as she spoke to Tony. "So, what now?"

His shrug was expressive. "Now, you get to die, unless..." He inclined his head toward the bedroom. "We could have some fun before you go. It might make your demise less—painful?"

She gave them both a look of contempt, shaking her head. "I'd rather die right now."

"That can certainly be arranged." Tony raised his pistol.

TWENTY-EIGHT

JIM MARVELED at the number of vehicles in his drive. The disabled SUV was still there, although it had been moved, along with a radio car sitting beside the road. A new van he hadn't seen before was pulled in front of the door. He saw Josh Barnes's Charger parked by the house, along with another patrol car.

They'd blacked out the windows earlier, but he could see shadows moving about through the open door and window he'd opened earlier. Something was off. It didn't feel right, and the open window was too exposed to look through. He moved to another window trying to see around the edge of black plastic taped there. He could hear voices but couldn't make out the conversation.

The only thing he could think of was going up through the trapdoor and hoping nobody was standing right there. That could be awkward—and deadly.

He was starting to move when the cold edge of a barrel pushed against his neck and he stopped. With a silent curse of self-admonition, he started to turn.

"Stop." The feminine voice was barely heard over his

pounding heart. Quick hands took his gun from its holster and then searched for other weapons. He knew the voice and felt like an idiot for allowing himself to be ambushed.

"Alina." He whirled, trying to catch her gun arm. All he got was air.

The pistol came back and was jammed into his abdomen. "Stop that, you damned fool."

They stood staring at each other for a moment in the near darkness before she continued. "Okay. Got your wits about you now? Be calm. Now, let's go join the party."

As they walked in, she shoved him in the back. He stumbled into Rita and grabbed her, looking her over. She watched Alina over his shoulder like someone mesmerized by a snake, wondering when it would strike. Seeing Barnes lying on the floor, he turned and watched a large man duck outside and then looked at Tony. He moved to stand in front of Rita. "You just couldn't leave it alone, could you, One-Ball? You've gotten a lot of men killed. And all for your worthless ego."

Tony smiled. "Cheap help is expendable." His expression turned malevolent. "As for you? You took something from me. Now, I'm going to take something from you."

He moved toward them. "Alina, it's good you showed up. Since you're here, you can hold a gun on lover boy. Play with him if you want. I'm going to take his woman into the bedroom and break her in. She looks fun. I bet she's a screamer."

They heard a slight coughing sound and the metallic clicking as the slide ejected a spent casing from the suppressed .22 Alina held. The shell caught the light and flashed as it tumbled to the floor. Tony followed the expended casing like a puppet with its strings cut. The hole in the back of his head leaked a small amount of blood on the floor.

Alina shrugged and met Jim's gaze. "You won't believe this, but I never liked him."

"You're right. I don't." He looked from her to the dead man. "Strange bedfellows?"

"I wish it weren't so, but he knew things about me. When you saw us together, it was not consensual. Call it blackmail, if you will. At the most, he was a necessary evil I put up with. Until lately, he was useful." She shrugged. "All things come to an end."

"And me? What was I? Would I have come to the same end as Tony?" He was still trying to get his mind around this new Alina.

Her shrug was eloquent this time and her expression pained. "I'm not a monster—I like to think I'm more of a soldier. After a job was done, you were my sanctuary— my piece of normal. If there was any blowback, I could count on you to protect me without question, at least for a while. I know a lot more about your talents than my father."

"Gee, thanks for the vote of confidence. And again, I don't believe you."

Her lips turned upward in a small smile before she spoke. "You look down on me as a killer? And what is the body count from this little exercise? I'd put it near twelve."

He shook his head, not conceding the point. "Some weren't mine, and I didn't start this."

"Still, we're not so different, you and me. My services are never called for until a conflict needs to end. We both do what needs to be done." Her smile didn't reach her eyes.

Before she could say anymore, Barnes stirred with a groan and tried to sit up. Alina pulled a stiletto and flipped it between Jim's feet. It quivered as the thin blade stuck in the floor. "Go ahead and cut him loose."

Jim helped Barnes to his feet while a mountain of a man walked into the room.

Alina's voice was cold as her gaze. "So, you thought all the times I was in Branson I was starring in some family play? Maybe a porno flick? I never expected you to be so dense."

Rita's voice broke in. "Maybe he was trusting. Trust doesn't expect betrayal, that's why it's so easy."

The two women stared for a moment, one hot with anger, the other cold and calculating.

"A smart person should always expect betrayal. Naivety doesn't help either party."

Half listening to the verbal sparring, Jim watched with morbid fascination as the giant enclosed Tony's head in a plastic bag and then sealed it shut with a zip tie around the neck.

Alina spoke to the man. "Thank you, Gregory."

The huge man looked at her a moment and then grabbed the body by the heels and dragged it outside. In the silence, they could hear Tony's head thumping down the porch steps.

As Rita helped a groggy Barnes find a chair, Alina spoke again. "I have another loose end to tie up. Perhaps you can help?"

She still held all the cards, not to mention the pistol. He moved to stand in front of Rita again. His perception was that Alina didn't like loose ends or let them live long. "Enough of this."

Alina shook her head. "So protective of her. I'm envious. I'm not going to kill your new girl. Now, where is Viktor?"

Jim relaxed as he watched her, waiting for a chance at her gun. "You may consider that loose end taken care of. He went spelunking. I don't think he was equipped for it."

She smiled at that, not needing an interpretation. "Nice. I'm too claustrophobic to muck around in caves. May I assume that is a permanent endeavor on his part?"

"A one-way trip." He took a deep breath before continuing. "Along with several players in the field, as Tony liked to put it."

Still keeping watch, she stepped away from them. Pulling out her cell phone, she made a call without looking. Her gaze never left Jim, and the gun didn't waver an inch from his chest. Maybe he should be flattered that she considered him the most dangerous. He was tempted since she held a small caliber pistol. But the risk of collateral injury behind him was too great.

When the call connected, her voice was soft. "It's done." A pause. "Yes, of course." Listening for a moment longer, she then terminated the call.

Alina stepped toward the door as Gregory came in with a wire brush, sponge, and spray bottle. After a scrub job, they watched in as he took a small bottle of alcohol from his pocket and poured it over the stain. He lit it on fire, watched a moment and then stamped it out. Once more, he sprayed the floor and cleaned it up. The floor was spotless in moments, showing no stain and leaving the stench of chlorine.

Jim couldn't resist. "Thanks, Gregory. I needed a more distressed-looking floor. They're all the style these days."

The man looked at him and he thought he saw a glint of humor in his eyes before the masked expression came back.

Alina's voice was calm as she spoke with no more emotion than she might use in a boardroom meeting. "Please listen to me. I'm sincere in this. Especially you, Mr. Barnes. My father wishes to convey a message. This matter is over. He is sorry for the trouble caused and that is a true apology. Tony initiated this whole fiasco because he felt disrespected, and then finished by bringing in Viktor as some sort of power play, wanting my father's position. That's not the way we want to do business. It's been tried before, with little success. His exact words were that he owes you one, and that means anything he can reasonably do. It was never his intention for things to turn out this way. I don't think any of us wants an escalation at this point. Agreed?"

Barnes replied in a weak voice, "Just like that? How can your father bargain? We have him in custody."

Her laugh was a sharp bark. "He was in custody for less than an hour. By the time the courts get to him, he'll be in a nursing home getting his diapers changed, and I'll be living on a beach someplace warm."

Barnes's voice was gaining strength. "Are there beaches in hell? Maybe they'll save a place for you next to your father."

"You should lighten up, Barnes. Hatred and anger never gives you anything but a bellyache." Alina gestured at the floor. "Besides, you have no evidence that I was ever here and your witnesses may not be reliable."

Turning to leave, she stopped and looked at Rita. "Take care of him. He's a good man." Her smile was soft for a moment. "And as you said, an honest man. Too bad." Her gaze pinned each of them a moment and then rested again on Rita. "I'll be watching."

Rita stepped forward. "Did you kill them?"

Alina looked puzzled. "Kill them? Who?"

"Agnes. The dispatcher. And Barney. If you did, I'll find you."

"Such bravado." They locked gazes a moment before Alina gave a slight smile. "I'm sorry for your loss, Rita. I am. For the record, I did not kill your friend Agnes or the deputy. I suspect that would have been Viktor."

She shrugged. "If I had killed her, I'd simply kill you now to neutralize the threat." She paused to look at all of them again, her gaze finally resting on Jim. "This will be a beautiful home one day. Enjoy it with your lady."

Jim limped to the door, listening to the sound of a vehicle leaving. When he turned back, Rita stood, shaking her head as she stared at him.

"You lived with an assassin?"

He shrugged. "Like I knew?"

Barnes staggered past them to the door and met his two men coming in. They were both talking at once until he told them he'd explain later. He turned at Rita's voice, momentarily losing his balance. One of his men grabbed his arm to keep him steady.

"Do you remember the little trick with my cell phone video?" She lifted it from her pocket. "What do you think?"

He looked at them a moment and then shrugged. "All things considered, I'd rather have Ivanov owe us a favor. He doesn't know it yet, but he's going to spend a boatload of money cleaning up the mess in White Rock. And I want to see his face when I return all these SUVs to his car lot. If by chance you can find where certain bodies disappeared, I'd donate them to the same place."

When there was no answer, he continued. "All right. Forget I asked. Jim, if I give you a day, can I open the area for tourists? We've told people not to come to this side of the lake to hunt or fish. I'd hate for someone to stumble onto something unsavory."

Jim nodded. "I understand. Give me two days."

Looking at his men, Barnes said, "Okay. We're outta here. I need to go to Mercy for x-rays of my head. My wife says there's nothing in there. Some days I think she's right. I'm getting too old for this. While I'm there, I'll check on Sally and let you know. Last report I had is that she'll pull through."

After they left, Jim closed and locked the door, for what good it did. Anyone with a pocket knife could get in.

Rita was looking him over. "You look like you've been through a meat grinder. We need to get you cleaned up." She shook her head at him. "We should have gone out with Barnes."

He was surprised when she got them naked and pulled him into the shower—and glad he'd built a big walk-in. Later, he sat on the edge of the bed as she applied ointment and then bandaged his wounds. The crease in his arm hurt and the wound on his hip was more of a nuisance than hindrance. The cuts on his leg worried him the most. There's nothing dirtier than the tusks on a feral hog, since they eat more dead flesh than a buzzard. He felt groggy as he reached for her.

Rita pushed him back on the bed and then pulled a sheet over them.

"Go to sleep, baby. When daylight comes, and if I can

find a vehicle that runs, you're going to the hospital for stitches and shots."

"Nope. Got some cleanup to do. Made a promise." He couldn't remember being so tired.

———

THE HOSPITAL ROOM was quiet with the steady beeping of a heart monitor the only noise. Sally stirred awake and looked around.

"How long have I been out?"

Jim rose and walked to the bed. "A few days."

"Dammit, there goes my vacation time." She looked past him. "Barnes, what are you doing here?"

He shrugged. "Nothing better to do. Just waiting for someone to take me fishing."

She gave him a puzzled look. "Why aren't you working?"

Barnes laughed at that. "My wife went to headquarters and turned in my resignation papers. She even signed them for me and dared me to object. My skipper accepted them because he was afraid of getting shot. Go figure."

Sally chuckled and then grimaced in pain. "Rita, you going to hurt me if I kiss your man? Just to tell him thanks?"

Rita came up and leaned over, kissing her on the forehead. "Not likely." She turned away and spoke over her shoulder. "Do your duty, Jim."

"So." Sally moved to a more comfortable position. "Highway patrol has his head wrapped in bandages, the Shepherd has more gauze on him than a runaway mummy, and I'm wired for sound in a hospital bed. Did we win or lose?"

Jim followed Rita's lead and kissed her on the forehead. "You rest easy. We got a win on this one."

She sighed, tears forming in her eyes. "And the innocents? All those people. Did they get justice?"

It took a moment for him to answer.

"No, no justice. There never is with something like this. But there was a reckoning. And in Viktor's case, he got to think about it all the way down."

A LOOK AT BOOK TWO:
BLOOD JUSTICE

A STORY OF HEARTBREAK, REVENGE, BETRAYAL, AND REDEMPTION.

Jim Lane is a man with a haunted past. And while a storm is brewing in a country pushing toward the last tick of the doomsday clock, all Jim wants is to be left alone to live out his life on beautiful Lake Stockton and fill his freezer with fish.

But when he happens upon a young girl picking up donations at a store—her father in a coma, beaten by a member of a local drug gang—he can't help but get involved. Everyone knows who did it, but no witnesses will come forward.

Launching into the underbelly of the county to make things right, nothing goes as planned and survival is uncertain. To make matters worse, his attention is divided between his rocky relationship with the sheriff, an ex-lover mafia assassin, and the draining preparation of his ranch for a possible global shutdown.

Can Jim quietly pull himself together to survive country-wide chaos and ensure bloody justice?

AVAILABLE MAY 2023

ABOUT THE AUTHOR

Darrel Sparkman is an award-winning author of novels, novellas, and short stories. He's been included in three western anthologies, worked as a feature writer for *Saddlebag Dispatches* and blogged a short time for *Sundown Press*. His ideas come from a diverse past of serving as a combat search and rescue helicopter crewman in Vietnam and volunteer Emergency Medical Technician First Responder. He has worked as a professional photographer, computer repair tech, and was once part-owner of a commercial greenhouse operation and flower shop.

Darrel is enjoying semi-retirement and finally has that job that wakes him up every day—with a smile on his face.